4/92

MADRID UNDERGROUND

by the same author

CHRISTMAS RISING
SATURDAY OF GLORY

MADRID UNDERGROUND

A Superintendent Bernal Mystery

David Serafin

ST. MARTIN'S PRESS
NEW YORK

Library of Congress Cataloging in Publication Data

Serafin, David.
   Madrid underground.

   I. Title.
PR6069.E6M3   1984   823'.914   84-13339
ISBN 0-312-50401-2

First published in Great Britain by William Collins Sons & Co. Ltd.

First U.S. Edition

10 9 8 7 6 5 4 3 2 1

For Katherine
Elena rides again!

Author's Note

*The characters in this novel are entirely
fictitious, but their activities are set in Madrid
during the real events of May to June 1977.*
                                        D.S.

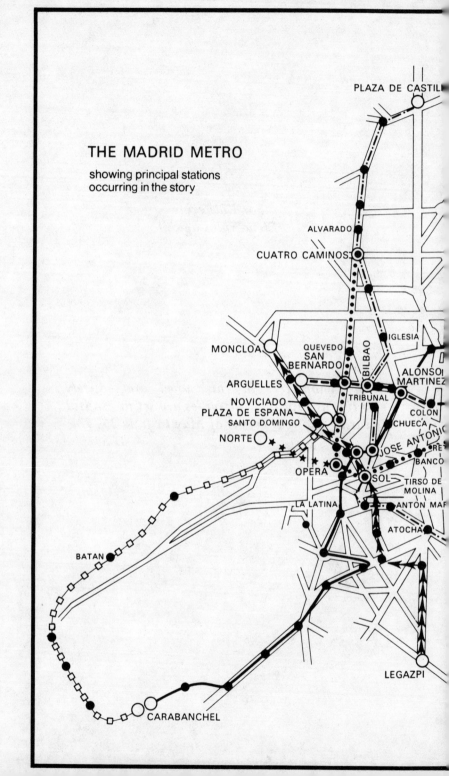

THE MADRID METRO

showing principal stations
occurring in the story

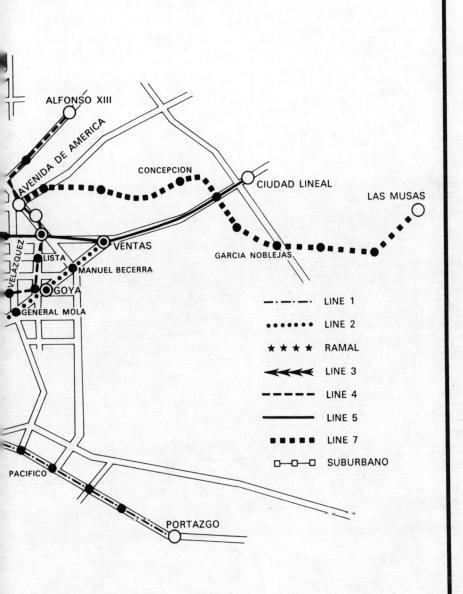

ALFONSO XIII

AVENIDA DE AMERICA

CONCEPCION

CIUDAD LINEAL

LAS MUSAS

VENTAS

VELAZQUEZ

LISTA

MANUEL BECERRA

GARCIA NOBLEJAS

GOYA

GENERAL MOLA

LINE 1
LINE 2
RAMAL
LINE 3
LINE 4
LINE 5
LINE 7
SUBURBANO

PACIFICO

PORTAZGO

ALFONSO XIII

The tall, broad-shouldered man stooped over the zinc hand-basin and let the stream of tepid water swill over the gleaming stainless-steel instruments. After wiping them dry with paper towels, he polished them carefully with a clean cloth and began replacing them in their exact fittings inside the large leather case.

He slipped the white latex gloves from his hands with practised ease, and scrubbed his fingers with a nailbrush. As he hung the white gown on the hook behind the door, he took one last look around to make sure everything was in order again, and climbed the concrete steps that led to the hallway.

There he stopped to listen, and heard only the regular rhythmic swing of the pendulum clock and the distant rumble of a Metro train far below the street outside. He locked the basement door and hid the key behind the decorative fretwork above the clock-face.

Despite his weight, he trod lightly up the carpeted stairs and stopped again on the landing, holding his breath. Satisfied there was no unusual sound, he unlocked the small door at the end of the darkened gallery and switched on the light in the small dressing-room. Inside, he removed his light overalls quickly, and began to don the carefully pressed dark blue shirt with the large patch pocket over the left breast, which bore a red, yellow and black insignia of yoke and arrows. Slipping into the wide-gusseted black trousers, he rapidly buckled the black belt to the penultimate hole.

Out of a drawer he took a plaited and tasselled red and black cord, which he attached from his right shoulder to the third button of the shirt-front. After brushing the collar, he slipped on a white military jacket, and straightened the medals as he inspected himself in the tall looking-glass. His chest swelled with pride as he glimpsed in his reflection more than a passing resemblance to his Nationalist idol, José Antonio Primo de Rivera.

Pushing open the door leading to the main room, he switched on the spotlights and paused to put on the gramophone record. He then marched to the far end of the room, drew back the red velvet curtains, and stood to attention before the red and gold national flag that bore in its centre the quartered shield of castles and lions rampant on a sable ground. On each side of it the spotlights illuminated a large gold-framed portrait.

As the somewhat scratchy strains of the Falange anthem, 'Cara al sol—Face to the sun', filled the room, the tall uniformed figure thrust out his right arm in the fascist salute, then bent and kissed the flag. Making a neatly executed quarter turn to the left, he gave the same salute to the left-hand portrait, crying out against the exultant music: '¡José Antonio Primo de Rivera, presente!' Then, clicking his heels once more, he turned to the right-hand portrait, fighting back hot tears, and made a third salute: '¡Viva Franco! ¡Arriba España!'

MONCLOA

It was the last Sunday in May, a fortnight before the first general election to be held for forty years, and it was cool and rainy for the season. Thousands of cars, coaches and motor-cycles were streaming out of Madrid past Moncloa, with klaxons blaring, and the hammer and sickle and the purple, red and gold banner of the Second Republic were being waved from every other vehicle, as hundreds of thousands of left-wing supporters made their way to the day-long Communist Party concentration at Torrelodones, which had been well advertised in the press for many days past. The advertisements had promised a million fried sardines, half a million barbecued lamb cutlets, speeches from revolutionary leaders such as La Pasionaria and Santiago Carrillo, and popular music to be rendered by Juliette Gréco and other guest artists to enliven the proceedings. The national railway company, the RENFE, was running special trains from Norte Station, and where the railway line ran near the road, the entrained and the motorized exchanged joyful waves and gave the clenched-fist salute.

Not that they were all, or even mostly, communists, by any means. It was simply the first public demonstration by the Left since Madrid fell to General Franco in 1939, and even then the new Government had been careful to sanction it only many kilometres from the capital. All those with the slightest liberal inclination, young and old, had arranged to be transported there, by any available means, as though this was a party that no one could afford to miss. The older people felt their veins swell as they sensed that spirit of a Popular Front, a euphoria of the common people, however short-lived they feared it would be. Just for this day they were determined to cock a snook at forty years of Francoism, although as it turned out there were no forces of public order in sight at whom to direct it.

As usual, the Deity proved to be on the side of the right-wing battalions of the *Búnker*. The latecomers, nearing the wind-swept field at midday, were astonished to encounter many others on their way back to Madrid.

'It's been cancelled!' some of these shouted through the confusion of traffic. 'Because of the rain! The field's flooded!'

Nevertheless the voice of the Party Secretary could be

heard booming distortedly over the loudspeakers, announcing that La Pasionaria would not be coming as planned as it was feared that her helicopter wouldn't be able to land safely. One of the singers who had offered their services free of charge then began to regale the rain-soaked crowd with a political song from the latest charts, and the cheerful *militantes* or party workers began to serve the cutlets and sardines from improvised tables. It was like 1936 all over again.

CUATRO CAMINOS

The *taquillera* at Cuatro Caminos Metro station paid little attention to the heavily built, bearded man whose hat and pulled-up raincoat collar hid his features almost entirely. She thought it slightly odd that he should ask for one single and one return: at twenty to nine in the morning, nearly every traveller took a worker's return for eight pesetas, a concession that was only available up to 9 a.m. The person he seemed to be supporting — she couldn't tell if it was a man or a woman — was equally muffled up. Of course it was rather cool for late May, and it was raining, she thought to herself, but these two must really feel the cold.

As the strange pair went through the metal barrier, she caught a glimpse of the person being supported — dragged along, almost, she noted — with the feet twisted and dangling free. Perhaps it was one of the crippled beggars, being taken to his or her pitch in one of the Metro stations in the centre of the city, to be placed in one of the underground hallways with a pathetic note pinned to the coat and a collecting-tin set between the useless legs.

The tiled walls of the station were completely plastered

with election propaganda. Every night teams of youths laboured feverishly throughout Madrid with buckets of paste and large brooms: she had heard that some of the newly formed political parties were paying them as much as a thousand pesetas each a night, or eight pesetas per poster, to proclaim the desirability of joining the PSP, PSOE, PCE, FDC, UCD, AP—she couldn't remember all the initials, let alone what they stood for. My God, what a change in six months, she reflected. She seemed to have spent all her life issuing tickets for a miserable pittance in this draughty hall, with evil-smelling water seeping through the roof even during dry summers. During Franco's régime the white wall-tiles had always been bare, apart from the accumulated grime from the traffic fumes which blew down the stairs. Then last December, with the referendum on the constitutional reform, the bill-sticking had begun: 'Vote Yes!' 'Vote No!' 'Abstain from the capitalist referendum!' 'Franco would have voted No!'

When the special cleansing teams had finally managed to scrape off the worst of the referendum bill-sticking, the Government declared 15 June as Election Day, and the posters and stickers returned with greater intensity than before. The *taquillera* or woman ticket-clerk quite liked the six Communist posters bearing a sepia photograph of La Pasionaria which faced her ticket-office; she remembered when she was a child being taken to the Puerta del Sol to see Dolores Ibarruri appear on the balcony of the Gobernación, during the last year of the Civil War, and to hear her shout her famous slogans: '*¡No pasarán!*—They shall not pass!' '*¡Más vale morir de pie que vivir de rodillas!*—It's better to die on your feet than live on your knees!' Well, *they* had passed, and *she*'d been right about the knees bit. The *taquillera*'s mouth tightened bitterly as she recalled how, less than three years before, the Metro workers had gone on strike at Christmas for more pay and Franco had 'militarized' them within four days. Her invalid husband had been amused, at first, at her conscription into the army.

She also liked the PSOE or Workers' Socialist Party poster, alongside the Communist one, showing a young, virile-looking Spanish emigrant getting off a train with a suitcase — returning from France or Germany, she supposed — and the slogan 'Put an end to emigration! Vote Socialist!' She thought she would; La Pasionaria was past it now, and that young Socialist leader Felipe González was a nice-looking chap in a working-class kind of way.

Further down the stairs, along the southbound platform of Line 2, the previous night's bill-sticking had reached a new peak: the large official billboards advertised Manuel Fraga's right-wing Alianza Popular, but the unofficial bill-stickers had clearly turned the empty space on the huge yellow posters to their own advantage, so that they now read 'Put an end to corruption and dishonesty — *Vote for the Workers' Socialist Party!*'

The passengers waiting for the train which had arrived at the opposite platform to go into the tunnel and re-emerge on the up-line were too engrossed in reading the wall propaganda to notice the large, bearded man supporting the disabled person against the tiled wall. When the train came in, there was a fairly orderly rush for the doors, but the burly man managed to get two seats in the last but one coach and arranged his companion on the seat facing him. The cripple sat with bent head, lolling against the window, and nothing could be seen of the face, which was covered by a grey felt hat and the turned-up collar of the coat.

The whistle blew, and the automatic doors closed, and the ancient red-and-cream train trundled out of Cuatro Caminos station.

QUEVEDO

It was a longish run to the next station, Quevedo, and the train picked up speed. The bearded man appeared to help his companion into a more comfortable position from time to time. When the train drew in at the platform and the doors opened, the coach started to fill up.

SAN BERNARDO

After the short run to San Bernardo station, a number of people got off in order to change to Line 4. Now more passengers than ever crammed into the train. The smell of wet mackintoshes increased, mingling with the residual odour from the mouths of those who had had a garlic sandwich for breakfast and the aroma of black tobacco from the smokers who had dowsed their cigarettes on entering—'Smoking or carrying a lighted cigarette forbidden: 5 pesetas fine,' warned the large pre-war notices in each carriage; 'Selling not permitted in the coaches.'

Hanging tightly together on the ceiling-straps, the commuters tried to read folded newspapers, or examined one another discreetly out of the corner of their eyes. A gaggle of schoolgirls chatted and giggled in the centre of the carriage, without sparing a glance for the bearded man and the bent figure seated opposite him.

NOVICIADO

At Noviciado, the next station on Line 2 southbound, yet more travellers strained into the coaches, until there was a solid press. One of the schoolgirls looked round suspiciously at the middle-aged man standing behind her, wondering whether it was just his briefcase that was touching her buttocks. Her friends nudged her knowingly, and they all burst into laughter once more.

SANTO DOMINGO

As the train approached Santo Domingo, some passengers struggled to reach the doors, asking those blocking their way, in cross tones, '¿Va a salir? — Are you getting out?' When the doors opened, there was a minor upheaval, and a steady movement of preparation for the arrival at the next station, where the major battle between alighters and boarders would take place.

ÓPERA

At the major interchange station of Ópera, under the Teatro Real in front of the Royal Palace, there was so much confusion that no one noticed the burly, bearded man slip out of his seat and make for the door. The enormous lady who immediately plonked herself in the vacated seat paid no attention to the strange figure whose legs dangled over the edge of the wooden seat without touching the floor and whose face was pressed against the window-pane.

SOL

The train almost emptied at Sol station, which was the hub of the whole underground railway system, and the stout lady spread her shopping-bags around her more comfortably. More passengers entered the train for its journey eastwards to Ventas, the other end of the line.

The type of traveller had now changed: there were a number of uniformed bank messengers, who would be getting off at Sevilla or Banco, and a few military personnel on their way to the War Ministry or the Ministerio de la Marina at Cibeles, above Banco station. The other passengers crowding the interior of the coach began to press against the stout lady and the lolling figure of the cripple.

RETIRO

Soon after Banco, the train began to climb the snaking tunnel under the Calle de Alcalá and chugged its way to Retiro. There, on the opposite platform, waiting for a train from Ventas to Sol, a short, rather paunchy man in his late fifties, whose close-cut moustache resembled that of the late General Franco, paced impatiently up and down. Superintendent Luis Bernal was annoyed that he had overslept, more particularly because he had to present a homicide case to the examining magistrate at 10 a.m.

Bernal's wife Eugenia had gone to her ancient farmhouse in Salamanca Province for a few days, and his younger son Diego, the only other member of the family at home, was in a deep stupor from his night on the tiles. Bernal had tried in vain to get him up for his first lecture at the University, but he had simply groaned and turned over. Without time for his usual breakfast in Félix Pérez's bar at the corner of his street, Bernal felt deprived.

MANUEL BECERRA

The red-and-cream train chugged onwards to General Mola and Goya stations without incident. But as it picked up speed on the run to Manuel Becerra, the stout lady encumbered with shopping-bags was alarmed to see the figure of the cripple begin to keel over.

Before she could put out her hand to save him, he pitched on his head on the floor of the train, and the hat fell off, revealing what was clearly a brown wig. The head lay at an extraordinary angle, and, as the plump lady released her hold on her bags to help the fallen traveller, a dark red pool began to form, as blood frothed out of the cripple's mouth. The stout lady screamed, and other passengers came to her aid.

As she lifted the head of the prostrate figure, more blood poured out on to her hands, causing her to scream again; but it was the strange touch and the curious lightness of the head and arms that sent her into hysterics.

'Oh dear Christ! Look at the blood! Oh, it's all over my hands! And, and—' she broke off with a sob, then a screech, which made all the remaining passengers in the coach turn to look at her, —'it's not . . . real! Not real!'

She plumped into her seat, sobbing and trying vainly to wipe the blood off her hands with a handkerchief, while a young worker in dungarees came over and lifted the cripple with ease, and opened the raincoat. As the other passengers gathered round, craning to see what was causing the stout lady to scream and sob so, the worker began to laugh.

'It's just a prank,' he said. 'It's a tailor's dummy dressed up in a raincoat and hat.'

'But the blood,' wailed the fat lady. 'How do you account for that?'

'The head's made of wax, and someone has put a container of something inside the mouth, so that when it fell off the seat, the red liquid would pour out. It's just a joke.'

'A bloody awful joke,' retorted the stout lady, giving vent to her feelings. 'I could have had a heart-attack.'

The other passengers bent to look at the dummy, as the train pulled into Manuel Becerra station.

'Call the guard, and the station-master,' suggested one of the passengers.

The station-master came from his glass-panelled office, and, on seeing what appeared to be blood on the floor of the coach, ran back to telephone the signalmen at Line 2 Central Control. The line was temporarily halted and the passengers were asked over the platform loudspeakers to alight and wait for the next train. The guard and the driver went back to the coach and asked the stout lady and the young worker to go to the office to await the arrival of the Metro security officer.

The doors of the train now containing only the blood-stained dummy were closed, and after a further consultation with the central signalling control, it was taken out of service to the coach-sheds at the next station, Ventas, which was the terminus of Line 2.

Two security officers from Sol Central Control got on to the next available train on Line 2 to travel to Ventas coach-sheds, but they were held up for a while by the temporary halt on the line. They got off at Manuel Becerra to question the station-master, who was making a cup of instant coffee laced with brandy for the stout lady, who, still surrounded by her shopping-bags, appeared to be coming out of shock and starting to enjoy being the centre of attention.

'Oh, I've never had such a fright! Really terrible it was! All that blood over my hands! It makes me shudder to think of it! Look, look, it's stained my coat. Will the Company pay for it to be dry-cleaned?'

'Of course, madam, the Company will see to everything. But can you tell us exactly what happened?' asked the older security officer.

'She looked odd to me from the start, I can tell you.' She was relishing giving this largely invented account. 'Strange way she looked at me, you know. I thought to myself, "That's a strange sort of beggar, lolling her head against the window." And why didn't she get off at Sol where most of the beggars go?'

'But did you see anyone with her, or rather, it?' asked the security man.

'No, no. She just sat there and glowered at me, until she fell off the seat, that is.'

'What made you think it was a woman?' continued the security man.

'I don't know,' she admitted hesitantly, realizing that she had not really looked at the figure until it fell down and the hat fell off revealing the wig of light brown hair. 'She . . . she seemed too small to be a man.'

'But it could have been a boy?'

'Yes, I suppose so. I didn't pay much attention, to tell you the truth. Can I go home now?'

'Yes, of course, but we'd like you to make a statement first.'

'All right, but I've got a lot to do. Will I get compensation for the shock?'

'The Company Chairman will study the matter, señora, you can be sure.'

'What about a free season-ticket?' she demanded.

'We'll certainly tell him that you'd like one,' said the security man.

VENTAS

At the terminus, the coach containing the dummy had been uncoupled from the rest of the train by a complicated manœuvre, and the rest of the train reformed with a spare coach.

The two Metro security officers arrived at the *cocheras* and were led to the coach which was now isolated in a siding, with its doors open. They examined the dummy, and sniffed the blood or red liquid.

'It smells of plastic,' said the younger man. 'It's quite realistic, isn't it?'

'With modern paints you can do anything,' said the older man. 'The dummy isn't one you'd find in a shop window, is it? It's quite light and made of polystyrene or some such substance.'

'But the face and hands are heavier,' the younger man pointed out. 'They've got a covering of real wax, and they've been painted to give a more natural finish. Any labels on the clothes?'

'The one on this old raincoat has been cut off. The hat is an old man's hat, like the ones we used to wear in the 'fifties. The rest of the clothes are old rags.'

'Have you ever come across a thing like this before?'

'Only at Carnival time, when people tend to cart those giant papier-mâché heads into the trains, especially at La Latina and Lavapiés stations, but I've never seen such a realistic lifesize job as this. Just a sick joke to make the women scream, that's all,' said the older man.

'Shall we inform the police? It'll be the Ventas Comisaría, which is just above us in the Calle del Cardenal Belluga, isn't it?'

'I don't think there's any need. Anyway, the Comisaría's moved from there. We'll just make out a Company incident report, and let the Head of Security decide. We'll put this dummy into storage here, and let them clean up the train.'

IGLESIA

Arminda Santiago, a neurotic woman in her early fifties, was on her way to her weekly consultation with her psychiatrist. Perched on the edge of a seat in the third coach of the Metro train on Line 1 southbound, she clutched nervously at her handbag as the ill-dressed and evil-smelling beggar opposite her suddenly leant forward when the train picked up speed leaving Ríos Rosas station. When the sudden braking on the descent to Iglesia launched the beggar on top of her, she began to yell, and her yells turned to hysterical screams as he began to gurgle blood on to her face and dress.

The other passengers came to her aid, and pulled the beggar away from her. The soldier who came up first exclaimed, 'But it's a doll! It's not a person, it's a doll!'

The others craned over his shoulder, and one woman began to laugh. As the train slowed and came to a halt at Iglesia station, Arminda's cries and feeble attempts to wipe the blood off with her handkerchief grew more frenzied.

'Call the police!' she screamed. 'It's murder! It's murder!'

The onlookers tried in vain to calm her, and finally the station-master led her to his office and telephoned Metro Security. The train was taken out of service, and, after Line 1 had been temporarily put out of action, it was returned to Cuatro Caminos coach-sheds to await inspection.

CUATRO CAMINOS

The same two security men gazed in fascination at the second dummy they had seen in a week.

'It's very similar to the last one,' said the younger man. 'Only it's been made to look more like a man this time. Who the hell can be doing it?'

'Medical students playing a joke on us, I'll bet,' said the older man.

'Should we call in the police?'

'We'll recommend it to the Chief. Otherwise that woman having hysterics in Iglesia station will let all hell loose and call the newspapers. The Company won't want the publicity, however daft it all is. Whoever is doing it manages to make the blood look very realistic, doesn't he?'

PACÍFICO

In the new and shining block which housed the head-quarters of the Madrid Metropolitan Company in the Calle de Cavanilles, the Head of Security read through the two reports on the dolls found in the trains with great puzzlement. The Company was having the worst year of its existence. Since it began with the support of King Alfonso XIII in 1919, it hadn't made a loss until 1976, even though in recent years successive governments had not permitted it to put up the fares to a realistic amount. As a result it had cut back on renovation of rolling-stock, stopped work on three extra sections of line under construction, and was facing a huge deficit, which the shareholders would certainly scream about. Though it was strictly not his province, he thought it absurd that the single fare, any distance, should be pegged at six pesetas, and the worker's return at eight, when the buses were much dearer.

He wondered whether these dolls were just a sick joke. The artificial blood was a novel feature. Perhaps an attempt to cause panic among the passengers? A thought suddenly crossed his mind: what if the blood was real, and human at that? Perhaps he should get a sample taken from each doll for analysis, just in case. He made a mental note to have it done the next day, and left his office to go to lunch.

ANTÓN MARTÍN

María Rosa Pérez snuggled into the corner seat in the old Metro train, and shook the water off her rain-hat from the heavy shower she had run through on coming out of the Roxy Cinema. She had enjoyed seeing Buñuel's *Viridiana*, so long banned in Spain, but she was feeling guilty at getting home late to cook her husband's supper. Alberto, she knew, would still be clearing up in the bar at a quarter to midnight, but it would take her some time to get from Vallecas station to their flat in the Avenida de Monte Igueldo. She was aware that her husband never ceased to be amazed at her liking for arty films and avant-garde plays, but old habits died hard with her, and although she had make a working-class marriage, her mother had been a famous film star in the rather insipid folklore films made in the 'thirties, and had surrounded her with all the bric-à-brac of a cultured home.

María Rosa pulled her fur-collared coat more tightly around her, and gazed at the graffiti scrawled on the wall at the end of the coach. '*Queremos una piscina en la Calle del Pingarrón*—We want a swimming-pool in Pingarrón Street,' begged the first scrawl. Well, it was a noble wish for the very poor and neglected suburb of Entrevías, she thought.

'*La vida es una barca. Firma: Calderón de la Mierda*—Life is a boat. Signed: Calderón of the Shit,'

opined the second scrawl. Rude and literary at the same
time, María Rosa noticed, with its modification of the
title of Calderón de la Barca's play *La vida es
sueño—Life's a Dream*. Obviously, surrealism was
reaching out into the sub-real world of the poorest and
most outcast of the city.

Up until now, Señora Pérez had paid little attention to
the ill-dressed girl on the seat opposite her, who appeared
to be sleeping with her head resting against the window of
the carriage. When María Rosa had got on at Bilbao
station, after a long wait due to the infrequency of the
service at that hour, she had cast an inquisitive eye over
the girl, who at that moment was the only other
occupant. Very pale, she looked, with her left hand
dangling below the seat. Perhaps she was a drug-addict?
She certainly didn't take care of her appearance, with a
dirty red scarf tied round her unkempt hair.

As the train rocked through the tunnel between Tirso
de Molina and Antón Martín stations, where the line
curved sharply to the east, the ill-dressed girl suddenly fell
in a heap on the floor. María Rosa got up to help her as
three youths who had got on at Sol looked curiously on
from the far end of the coach.

'Are you all right?' she began to ask the girl. Then she
spotted the blood coming from her mouth. María Rosa's
gorge rose, but she checked her incipient scream and was
sensible enough to feel the girl's pulse. The wrist was
quite limp and clammily cold, warning Señora Pérez that
she had a corpse on her hands.

As the train entered Antón Martín station, she shouted
to the three youths to get the guard from the first coach
and the station-master. When these officials saw the
body, they rang through to Sol Central and the service on
Line 1 was suspended.

RETIRO

Superintendent Bernal was just dropping off to sleep when the phone rang just before 1.30 a.m. His wife Eugenia was still away in Ciudad Rodrigo, seeing to her almost barren lands and poverty-stricken tenants, and would no doubt arrive at the end of the week bearing hams, cheeses, sausages, olives or other produce which she extracted in lieu of rent. Diego, their younger son, still hadn't come home. He was probably at the Boccaccio discothèque, thought Bernal. At least he hoped he was. He'd rather he sowed his wild oats there than in a pot party or even worse, in the flat of one of the wilder members of the Faculty.

The duty officer was apologetic. 'I wouldn't have called you, sir, but the group on duty has been called to a domestic homicide in San Blas. And your group is next on the list.'

'Very well. Where's the scene?'

'In Antón Martín Metro station, sir. A young girl dead on the train. Strange features in the case, according to the District Inspector.'

'Would that be Arévalo?' Bernal remembered the rather stiff-backed and right-wing Inspector from previous cases.

'That's right, sir. He wanted the Directorate General of Security in at once.'

'Then there must be something strange about it,' said Bernal, with some irony. 'Would you call Navarro and Miranda for me and tell them to meet me at Antón Martín?'

'But the train had to be taken to the end of the line at Portazgo, sir, in order not to interrupt the last services on Line 1. The Metro is closing for the night now, but Inspector Arévalo and the Metro chief security officer will meet you at Portazgo station.'

'Can you send a car for me?'

'It's already on its way, sir. I thought—' the duty officer hesitated—'I had no doubt you would come out if you could.'

'That's very kind of you,' said Bernal ambiguously. 'I'll be getting dressed.'

PORTAZGO

Inspector Miranda had arrived before Bernal, since he lived in Vallecas suburb, and he was already taking a statement from María Rosa Pérez, who was obviously anxious to get home.

Bernal questioned her briefly, then told his driver to take the lady home.

'We'd better ask Dr Peláez to come out,' he said to Arévalo. 'This is a very odd case. The girl's corpse is cold, as you've noticed, but rigor mortis has not set in. Yet blood poured from her mouth. I suppose it is real blood? It looks remarkably light-coloured.'

'I'm not sure, Superintendent,' said Inspector Arévalo. 'It's certainly cold to the touch, and has a faint smell of nail varnish.'

'If it's real blood, why isn't it congealed, or even drying?' asked Bernal. 'Peláez and Varga will have to do some tests. Was she carrying a handbag?'

'Not as far as we can see, and Señora Pérez didn't see one.'

Bernal looked through the witnesses' statements. The three youths who had been made to travel to the end of the line had added nothing and knew even less than the woman.

'Señora Pérez's a respectable woman, wife of a bar-owner and daughter of a cinema actress of the 'thirties,' said the district inspector. 'Quite a good witness, I'd say.'

'And the dead girl was already in this seat when she got on at Bilbao?' Bernal observed that the seat had an old-fashioned metal notice alongside it proclaiming that it was reserved for 'mutilated people and invalids'.

'Yes, and she was propped against the window. Señora Pérez naturally thought at first that she was asleep.'

The coach was of the oldest R series, almost certainly pre-war, thought Bernal, and it had the usual paper notice pasted on the end windows of each carriage, certifying that it had been 'disinsectified' during the previous month.

'Isn't the head of Metro Security here yet?' he asked Arévalo.

'They're having difficulty in contacting him. He and his wife went out to a dinner party, apparently.'

Peláez, the police pathologist, arrived breathless, eyes sparkling with interest behind his thick pebble lenses, and took over the examination.

'H'm, dead for some hours, though no rigor yet. Curious, this blood. Ha, plastic bag in mouth.' He pulled it out with tweezers. 'That's how it was done. As she fell off the seat, bag opens and out pours the blood. Why, eh? Why? To frighten people, eh? But it would be frightening enough for most people to have a *fiambre* fall on top of them.' Peláez's life naturally revolved round *fiambres* — 'cold meats' or 'stiffs'.

'But what did she die of?' asked Bernal.

'Ah, too soon to say. No obvious marks,' said Peláez, turning the corpse over and loosening the drab and dirty clothing. 'Probably not strangled. Suffocated? Could be. We'll have to cut her open to see. Coming along, Bernal?'

'No, no thanks,' said Bernal hastily.

'You'll get my report in the morning. Want finger-prints, I suppose?'

'Yes, as soon as you can, Peláez, since there doesn't seem to be any identification.'

SOL

The next day Bernal and Inspector Francisco Navarro, the most senior member of his group, puzzled over Peláez's report. The blood that poured from the mouth was real after all, but was mixed with a thinning substance, similar to that used in nail varnish, plastic paints and typing correction fluid. Presumably to keep it in liquid state. That accounted for its light appearance. The girl, who was aged between eighteen and twenty-two, had dark brown hair which was dyed blonde, brown eyes, pencilled eyebrows drawn higher than her shaved natural ones, a snub nose, wide mouth and good teeth. She was of slim build, not a virgin, well fed and cared for, probably lower middle-class, worked as a typist to judge by the small callouses on the outer edges of her thumbs.

The annular finger of her left hand bore a pale mark left by a largish ring, probably not a wedding ring considering the shape of the mark. The old clothing she was found in was almost certainly not her own; it bore no labels or marks, but it would be checked under black light for invisible laundry marks by Varga in the technical lab.

Cause of death uncertain, possibly asphyxiation, but the stomach contents, lungs, liver, kidneys and brain, as well as blood samples, would be examined by the Institute of Toxicology for signs of drugs or poison.

'Nothing to go on yet,' said Bernal crisply. 'If her prints are not in the criminal files, it may take weeks for Fingerprints to trace her right thumb and index finger in the complete national DNI files. What do you suggest, Paco?' he asked Navarro.

Inspector Francisco Navarro, Paco to his friends, was a meticulous reader of the small print and could be relied on to do a thorough check of reports and dossiers; he also possessed a marked procedural ability, even though he disliked working in the field himself.

'We could start by interrogating all the Metro station *taquilleras* who were on duty last night. They should have noticed someone carrying a corpse in. The girl must have been killed somewhere else some hours before and then was dumped on the train. We could do the stations on Line One first, *jefe*. It's not likely the killer would have changed trains.'

'That's true, Paco. And we could narrow it to the stations from Bilbao northwards, since the train was travelling south and Señora Pérez saw the corpse already in position when she got on at that station.'

Navarro walked along the platform and consulted the large plan of the Metro system in its glass case on the wall.

'That leaves only eight stations, chief, from Iglesia to the Plaza de Castilla.'

'But the ticket-clerks on duty last night will be at home now. We'll ask Metro Security for their addresses, and we'll deploy Lista, Miranda and Elena Fernández.' Carlos Miranda had been with the special homicide group for seven years, and was a phenomenal shadower of suspects; Lista was younger, tall, broad-shouldered and stolidly peasant-like, and this appearance made his brilliant flashes of intuition unexpected; Elena Fernández had been seconded to Bernal's group for only two months, but she had already shown herself to be thorough and to use intelligent initiative in difficult situations.

'You could send Elena to interview any of the female Metro staff if any of them were still on duty at that late hour,' Bernal added. 'Let's hope Varga and the lab technicians come up with something from the girl's clothing.'

PACÍFICO

The Head of Metro Security took Bernal's call, and said he would track down the names and addresses of the ticket-clerks on the late shift between Iglesia and Plaza de Castilla stations. He suggested that they try at Bilbao as well, since it was one of the busiest on that stretch of the line.

While his secretary was checking with Metro Personnel, the security chief dug out the reports on the two lifesize dolls found the previous week and re-read them. Could there be a connection with the murdered girl? It couldn't have been easy for anyone to cart the two dolls into the underground unnoticed, let alone the corpse of the girl. He thought he'd better get photocopies made of the reports and send them over to Superintendent Bernal.

SOL

The next morning Navarro was opening the mail in the Group's grubby office in the Gobernación building as Bernal came in to work.

'Varga's on to something, chief. He got Prieto in Fingerprints to try out that new method of electron autography which was first used in Scotland by the Glasgow police. Apparently they use lead powder and X-ray photography and can pick up latent prints from the most difficult surfaces, such as human skin, postage stamps on letters, and clothing. Varga found no invisible laundry marks on the clothes the girl was dressed in, but Prieto spotted one partial fingerprint on the scarf she was wearing.'

'Can it be checked out?' asked Bernal.

'He says it's too partial to classify properly. He can't tell if there were any deltas or whorls really, but he's got enough to try poroscopy, since the pores between and on the ridges are as unique and individual as the whole fingerprint.'

'Have we used the method before?'

'Prieto says he's tried it out for experimental purposes, and he's prepared to have a go at it, if you can find the owner of the print.'

'You mean it can't be checked against the files?' asked Bernal.

'Oh no. He can't even tell which finger of which hand it's from, and we classify in the criminal files by right hand, thumb to little finger for the main division, and then the left hand for the subdivisions. But Prieto says poroscopy is only useful if you get your man and want absolute proof it's him by checking all the pores of his fingertips against the pores of the partial print.'

'Well, that doesn't get us much further,' commented Bernal. 'What about the shoes and the scarf and so on? Can't Varga check with the manufacturers and retail suppliers?'

'It's hopeless, he says. They are of the commonest sort and look as if they were picked up in the Rastro Sunday Market.'

'So the murderer kept the girl's own clothes. Why?' asked Bernal. 'To avoid possible identification of them by us? Or because he's some kind of clothes fetishist?'

Navarro now opened the report from the Institute of Toxicology. 'Here's something, *jefe*. Look at this. They've found chloroform in the lungs, and traces of cocaine in the bloodstream. Was she addicted to sniffing the stuff? Peláez found no injection marks on her arms or thighs.'

'She may have died of an overdose of ether,' mused Bernal. 'And she was probably a cocaine-sniffer into the bargain. You'd better check with Estupefacientes, Paco. It could be that she is on their files—they have 170,000 hard-drug addicts recorded in Madrid alone, out of the population of less than four millions. They could check her fingerprints against their records. It should certainly be quicker than the needle-in-the-haystack method of looking for her right index-finger and thumb prints in the National Identity Files.'

Inspectora Elena Fernández now arrived, looking coolly elegant in an ice-blue tight-fitting dress.

'*Buenos días, jefe*. Have you got work for me?'

Bernal had begun to admire her ability always to look collected and well groomed, even after a long day's investigation, or after a late night out with her boy-friend in the Costa Fleming.

'We should like you to go and interview some women ticket-clerks from the Metro at their home addresses this morning. You'd better read these reports on a girl whose corpse was found in an underground train at Antón Martín station last night.'

Navarro was now opening a large envelope sent over by messenger from the Metro headquarters.

'The security chief has sent us the names and addresses of the ticket-clerks who were on duty last night between Bilbao and Plaza de Castilla stations. He's also sent copies of two reports on human-size dolls found in the trains during last week. He wonders if there's any connection. He says the Company hopes you can keep this girl's death out of the papers.'

'We'll do what we can, but they must expect some publicity sooner or later. The witnesses will talk.'

Bernal read the two reports with avid curiosity. He noted that the two security men who had been called to deal with the dummies talked of 'red paint' or 'red dye' pouring from the mouths of the dolls. It would have to be checked at once.

'Paco, ring through to Metro Security and ask them to send those two dummies, if they still have them, to Varga's lab, handling them as little as possible. You and Elena had better glance at these reports, and Miranda can do so when he comes in. You could take three ticket-clerks each and ask them about anything suspicious; for example, someone who staggered along, supporting a sick or invalid person, during the past week. I'll stay on here until Lista and Ángel turn up.' Bernal was resigned to the odd hours kept by Ángel Gallardo, his youngest and handsomest inspector, but he was somewhat surprised by Inspector Lista's lateness. 'One other thing, Paco, would you ask the Metro Company if they could send us a large chart of the underground system? We've only got a small leaflet of it here.'

When they had left, Bernal studied the three reports and the plan of the Metro. The first dummy had been discovered just before Manuel Becerra station on Line 2, direction Ventas. The second had been found on Line 1, between Ríos Rosas and Iglesia stations, and the train was travelling southwards, direction Portazgo. The girl's cadaver had turned up just before Antón Martín station, also on Line 1, and the train was also going south towards Portazgo, but the witness Señora Pérez had seen it much earlier, at Bilbao station. There was a clear correspondence between the last two incidents. The ticket-clerks between the terminus at Plaza de Castilla and Bilbao might shed light on one or both of them. Could the first incident be tied in? A further study of the map made it clear to him. Line 2 interconnected with Line 1 only at Cuatro Caminos and Sol stations, and Cuatro Caminos was also the northern terminus of Line 2. Sol station as the point of ingress could be ruled out in the case of the dead girl, because Señora Pérez had noticed her fellow passenger earlier. Therefore the connection had to be Cuatro Caminos, assuming that one person was responsible for the two dummies and the dead girl, and that he or she hadn't changed trains at any interconnecting station. Bernal thought this very unlikely, especially in the case of the girl, who had weighed over forty kilos. And in the case of the dolls, would the perpetrator have taken the risk of being spotted, which changing trains would have involved?

Bernal now wrote the dates and times of the occurrences on a sheet of paper: three days between the planting of each of the dummies, and both incidents occurred in the morning, around 9 a.m. Two days between the second dummy and the murdered girl, and she had been dumped late at night, or rather, in the early hours of the morning. But she must have been killed three or four hours earlier, say between 8 and 9 p.m. Missing Persons would have to be checked, because if she lived with her family or with a friend, they might have reported her missing by this morning. The problem would arise if she lived alone. She might not then be reported for some days, until her employer made some enquiries.

Miranda now came in and Bernal set him to read all the reports and take the last three names of ticket-clerks on the Metro's list and go and interrogate them.

ALVARADO

Elena Fernández walked slowly up the steps leading out of Alvarado station, her eyes everywhere, noting the access to the platforms on Line 1 and the barriers outside the ticket-office. Up in the street she looked at the name and address again: Victoria Álvarez, Calle del General Perón. She walked up Bravo Murillo and turned into General Perón, looking for the number of the high apartment block. She was lucky and found Victoria bathing her semi-paralysed husband in their lightless basement flat.

Victoria's lip had a bitter curl, and a frightened look came into her eyes as Elena showed her her still new warrant card.

Had she seen anything odd in Cuatro Caminos station where she worked during the past week or so? She saw odd people and things every day, she said.

'All those beggars and hawkers, who pour into the Metro now, trying to get past my barrier without buying a ticket. I've got to keep a sharp look-out, I can tell you.'

Elena made sympathetic noises. 'Did you ever see anyone carrying or supporting someone else?'

'Well, those gipsy women carry three or four children down every day, pretending they're crippled, to dump them in Ópera or Sol and leave the poor things begging all day long in the gloom. Inhuman it is. And the blind lottery-sellers; their relatives sometimes help them down the steps.'

'But have you seen anyone with their feet dragging along behind them, perhaps?' asked Elena, remembering the dummies.

'Now you mention it, I do remember that one morning.'

Elena took out her notebook eagerly.

'About a week ago it was, one morning when it was raining heavily. I was on the early shift. A burly man with a beard, hat pulled down over his eyes, holding up an invalid—I'm not sure if it was a man or a woman, it was muffled up, you understand. I only noticed because he took one single and one worker's return. Odd that was, I thought. Wasn't the other one coming back?'

Elena tried to get her to remember the day precisely, but she knew it had rained heavily a week the previous Thursday, because she herself had got soaked waiting for a microbus on the Castellana on her way to work. Anyway, she could check with the meteorological station in the Retiro Park.

'How long have you worked at Cuatro Caminos station, señora?'

'Oh, since just after the war. From the time when my husband was injured at work. Damp old place it is; I catch terrible colds in the winter.'

'And you don't remember any other incident—last night, for example?'

'No, I'm afraid not.'

'Well, you've been very helpful, señora. We'll probably need an official signed statement later. I hope your husband will be better soon.'

Victoria thought the DGS must have changed a lot from the old days. Then they would have screamed the questions at her, as though she were a criminal, she thought bitterly.

SOL

At midday, Bernal was reading the latest reports from the forensic lab with astonishment. The dead girl's blood group was O positive, but the blood that had emerged from the plastic bag forced into her mouth was B negative. Whose was it then? He called Lista in from the outer office.

'Let's see if we can have a look at the two dummies, if they've sent them across. We'll need detailed tests done on the blood they contained. We must find out if it all belongs to the same group or not. But get Peláez on the phone for me first.'

After a short delay, Lista indicated through the glass panel that divided Bernal's office from the outer room that Peláez was on the line.

'Peláez? Bernal here. I don't know whether you've seen the report on the blood samples taken from the girl found in the Metro. Not yet? Well, they're from different groups. Where could the criminal have got the other blood from? Assuming he's not a mass murderer. From the University Faculty of Medicine or a hospital? Yes, we'll check it out. You've heard about the two dummies found on the Metro last week? No? Well, they had plastic bags in their mouths, containing what appeared to be blood, as well. I'll get it all checked out by the lab. I'll call you back if I need further help. *Hasta luego.*'

On replacing the receiver, Bernal called Lista back in.

'I want you to go to the Faculty of Medicine and the hospitals, and ask about possible thefts of blood from the blood banks. At the moment we are particularly interested in B negative, which is a very rare group. You'd better check the School of Anatomy as well, in case the students are taking it from corpses. It's a very long shot, but we must check it out.'

A bright-eyed, handsome young man sauntered in at that moment.

'Ángel,' exclaimed Bernal, 'where have you been all morning?'

'I had rather a late night, chief, in that new discothèque in Velázquez. On Vice-Squad business, of course. Is there something up?'

'You'll have to read all these reports,' said Bernal firmly, 'and then accompany me to Varga's lab to look at two dummies. I'll see you this evening, Lista, when you've finished checking out the blood banks. *Que tengas suerte* — I hope you have some luck.'

In his chaotic laboratory, Varga unwrapped the two dummies from the plastic sheets that covered them.

'I've put the clothes back on for you to see the general effect, Superintendent. We've taken samples of the blood from the plastic bags that were in the mouths and sent them for analysis. If it's human, I've suggested detailed checks of the Rh, MN and Hr factors, and a test for antibodies and signs of disease. That will help to give us a "blood-print" of the person or persons to whom it belonged, approximate age, race, state of health, etc. And we could match it pretty exactly with any other sample we find. The clothes are all old rags, as you can see, probably picked up in a junk shop or in the Rastro on a Sunday morning. The frames of the bodies are made of wire, covered with polystyrene, but the hands and face are genuine wax, painted to give a realistic effect. The eyes are glass and the hair is a cheap commercial wig in each case, easily obtainable from one of the big stores.'

Bernal examined the dummies carefully and lifted one of them. 'Very light to carry, eh, Varga? That must have caused difficulties in itself, when it came to seating the dummies in the train. People might have noticed how light they seemed. What about the wax and so on? Can the sources of supply be checked?'

Varga considered the question. 'The polystyrene is easily available; it's sold in sheets and is used for various purposes. The wire is of fairly thick gauge, such as is used by modellers or sculptors. The wax is a different matter. It's not the same as in church candles, for example. It's of a softer, more malleable type, used for moulding. An obvious place that uses it is the Museo de Cera, the new waxworks in the Plaza de Colón.'

'I'll get Ángel to go round there and talk to the director. Can you give him a sample to take with him, Varga?'

'Yes, of course, if you'll authorize me to cut a piece out of one of these dummies.'

'Naturally I will. Give him a painted portion, and the waxworks people can have a look at the paint as well.'

MONCLOA

Lista remembered the layout of the University City from his student days, but it seemed to have grown even larger. There were no signs now that it had been in the battle-lines throughout the Civil War, when the Republican defenders of Madrid fired from the Faculty of Philosophy and Letters at the Faculty of Medicine held by the Francoist insurgents. All the pre-war buildings had been gutted then, and the new buildings were elegant and functional, with pleasant walks between them. He sought the Dean of Medicine's office first and got guidance on all the departments where blood might be stored. From the list he made, he could see that it was going to be a long day, let alone the hospitals in the city which had their own blood-banks.

COLÓN

Ángel strolled nonchalantly along the Paseo de Recoletos, and like most *madrileños* had no eyes for the faded rose-lilac flowers on the judas-trees which were just giving way to the veined, cordate leaves, nor for the neat rows of red Dutch tulips, planted at great expense by the Ayuntamiento amid beds of sprawling orange calendulas. His dominant interest was in people, and his sharp, dark eyes swept the windows of the Café Gijón, where the first contingent of theatre people were breakfasting at the bar.

As he reached the Centro Colón, he did glance across at the three enormous and mysterious concrete blocks, partly covered with plastic sheeting, which were being constructed on the other side of the Plaza de Colón, soon to change its name from Columbus Square to the Gardens of the Discovery. He had heard that the vast sculptures were meant to represent the three caravels Columbus had sailed in on the First Voyage. The nineteenth-century statue of the Discoverer had been repositioned on the south-west corner of the square, appropriately facing west and towards the Calle de Génova, the street named after Columbus's alleged native city of Genoa.

He looked with curiosity at the kiosk outside the Centro Colón, which bore pictures of the interior of the waxworks. He had never been inside, though he was perfectly familiar

with the Río Frío, the large modern café above the Museo de
Cera, and with the Boccaccio discothèque behind it.

He entered in the normal way, paying the hundred-peseta
entrance fee and twenty-five pesetas for a programme, and
was immediately confronted by two wax figures of the King
and Queen. Don Juan Carlos seemed smaller and rather
younger than he really was, Ángel thought, while Doña
Sofía looked older and rather green. Why was it that painted
wax never quite caught the real complexion of human skin,
unless one saw it in a bad light? And there was plenty of that
further on, in the hall of show-business personalities, some of
whom were moving figures, who gestured and sang. He
passed the bull-fighting section, finding the bull the best
thing there, especially as it rushed out now and then from a
puerta de toriles, only to be dragged back ignominiously by
the underfloor mechanism. He was naturally attracted by
the gallery of crime, and thought he'd have a look at that
before seeking out the manager. After a brief perusal of the
tableaux of famous crimes — he thought the raid on the
Andalusian Express in 1924 the best done — he made his way
through the halls of politicians, artists and writers to the
director's office.

On seeing his DGS warrant card, the manager was
immediately helpful. Perhaps he'd like to see the work-
shops? Ángel accepted with alacrity, and was introduced
to one of the technicians. After listening to an account of
the modern techniques of making wax figures, Ángel
showed the technician the sample of painted wax Varga
had taken from one of the Metro dummies.

'Yes, it certainly looks like the wax we use, Inspector,
but then it is also used by artists for moulding, and by
embalmers in difficult cases, I believe. The painting is
not very well done,' he sniffed. 'We shouldn't find it
acceptable here. The paints aren't of the type we use.
More like ordinary oil-paints, I'd say.'

'Could you give me the name of the supplier of the wax,

and of the plastic materials you use?' asked Ángel.

'Of course, Inspector, but I expect you'll find they have quite a list of clients and of retail outlets in the large cities. The plastics are much more used, of course, in dentistry, shop-window mannequins and modelling of various kinds. There's been a complete revolution in materials in the past fifteen years.'

Back in the manager's office, Ángel asked whether he could have a list of the technical staff. 'Have any of them left you in recent months, or have you any reason to think that wax or other materials are being stolen?'

'No, none at all, Inspector, and our staff is very stable and loyal. I'll make discreet enquiries, of course, and let you know if I come across anything suspicious.'

RETIRO

At 8.30 that evening, Bernal emerged, with surprisingly sprightly step, at the top of the stairs at Retiro station. Just before he left the office, Lista had rung in to say he had found out nothing of importance at the Medical School or the hospitals, except that the blood they used was normally diluted with plasma to stop it from coagulating and then refrigerated. There was no sign of any having been stolen. Miranda and Navarro had learned nothing from the ticket-clerks about how the body or the dummies had been brought into the Metro trains, though Elena had found one *taquillera* who probably had seen a burly, bearded man, his face half hidden by a hat, taking the first dummy down at Cuatro Caminos. This helped to confirm his view that that station was the point of ingress in all three incidents. Ángel had not yet reported in, and neither the Fingerprints Sections of the Drugs Squad nor the

National Identity Files had yet been able to identify the dead girl. Missing Persons had been consulted in vain.

Yet Bernal was not dismayed. It was the sort of case, well outside the normal run of things, which had always fascinated him, and if the dummies should prove to be connected with the murder, it smacked of *grand guignol* as well. He invariably tried to form a mental image of the murderer he was pursuing, building it up slowly from the tiny traces such people inevitably left behind. In this case, Bernal already had the strong sense of being in contact with a very disturbed personality, surely a man, psychopathic in his grotesque behaviour, but who might well appear to be quite normal to those around him.

Out on the Calle de Alcalá the evening was dark and chill, with a hint of rain which was very unusual for late May. Bernal decided to have an apéritif, and turned into Félix Pérez's bar, where he ordered a Larios gin and tonic. He glanced at the copy of *Diario 16* he had just bought in the street from the cheerful *quiosquero*. Almost the entire issue was devoted to the formation of the twelve party coalitions which were going into the General Election on 15 June, and the front page concentrated on President Suárez's television speech the night before, in which he revealed he would be entering the electoral arena at the head of a new party, the UCD or Unión del Centro Democrático. This announcement had brought down upon his head an hysterical attack from the extreme right and a milder criticism from the left. Flicking over the pages as he sipped his gin and chewed an olive which the bar-proprietor had served him on a long wooden spoon, Bernal's eye was caught only by the centre-page spread about the French 'sewer gang', who had carried out the robbery of the century in Nice. He soon tired of reading the rather sensational account, and left the newspaper on the counter as he departed. It still wouldn't do for any of his colleagues to see him reading such a left-wing journal, and in any case, in the Salamanca quarter of the city, there was a definite risk he might be attacked by the extreme rightist Warriors of Christ the King just for carrying it under his arm.

As he turned from the Calle de Alcalá into his street, Bernal was very surprised to see his wife Eugenia, dressed in peasant black, staggering under the weight of a glass carboy protected by basket-work, and two large shopping-bags, and accompanied by two boys who couldn't have been more than eleven or twelve years old. They were also heavily encumbered, one with a large mountain ham slung across his shoulders, and the other with a medium-sized barrel, which at that moment he was resting on the pavement edge.

'Eugenia?' cried Bernal. 'Why didn't you let me know you were coming home today? I could have come to Chamartín station to meet you.'

'Oh Luis, thank God you've come,' she panted. 'Take this olive cask, will you? These two lads offered to carry the rest of the things from the RENFE underground station at Recoletos.'

'Why didn't you take a taxi from Chamartín, Geñita?'

'Oh, there was no need to throw money away, when I could get the local train almost to the door. Two soldiers helped me change trains.'

The two boys, speechless and red in the face from their exertions, looked relieved as Eugenia said, 'Here's the house. Just carry them into the hallway, will you, there's good lads?' And then, in a stage whisper to her husband, 'Luis, give them two *duros* each, will you?'

'Ten pesetas each, Eugenia?' Bernal exploded. 'For carrying those heavy things all that way? I'll have to give them more than that.' Fishing into his wallet, he came out with a hundred-peseta note, while Eugenia looked pained. 'Divide that between you, will you, lads?' They slunk off in obvious relief.

Luis remembered how his wife had always had an

amazing knack of persuading complete strangers to do the most unlikely things for her; it must be the result of the burning authority in her eyes and the apparent helplessness of her figure, he considered. Only she would have set out alone on an eleven-hour train journey, during which she had to make two changes, loaded with enough baggage for a Saharan dromedary.

'Well, Luis,' she said at last, with an air of satisfaction, as he helped her to load the lift, 'I've brought all the produce I could get. A whole *jamón serrano*, a cask of olives, a carboy of that red wine you like, a Manchegan cheese and two strings of *chorizo* sausages. Think how much money we'll save on food! Have you been busy while I've been away? And did you take Diego to Mass regularly?'

'Diego's been very busy with his studies, Geñita.' Luis thought it wise not to mention his younger son's nocturnal escapades, to which he'd turned a blind eye. 'And I've got a very unusual case on.'

As they ascended in the ancient hydraulic lift, which had a polished mahogany cabin with a full-length bevelled mirror at the back and folding doors with brass handles, Bernal looked at Eugenia's haughty, beaked nose and burning dark eyes, and wondered once more how he had ever been attracted to her all those years ago in her native village.

Although as a callow young cadet in the Civil Guard he had not dreamed of analysing his feelings for her, even at this late date he was sure they had not included love in the conventional sense. She had been like a wild colt waiting to be broken in, and he now realized he had wanted above all to dominate her, to mould her to his ways, to the ways of the city. She was a countrywoman to her fingertips. Her father, a petty landowner, had regarded Bernal as beneath them socially, despite his promising start in the Civil Guard. And it was true. He had been the third son of an assault guard in the Republic, who was later to be killed in a street riot in

1936. Luis had never asked Eugenia what had attracted her to him; it couldn't have been his looks, since he was short, and even in his early twenties had a tendency to a paunch; his early attempts to cultivate a moustache must have seemed comic. Perhaps it was the lure of a sophisticated man of the city—the capital she had never visited.

What a disillusion he had suffered on his wedding night! The fire in Eugenia's eyes which he had taken to be sensual, turned out to be directed towards God. He realized how mistaken he had been to think her assiduous religious observance was natural in a teenage girl of her background and place. It was really her consuming passion, and remained so. Although she performed her marital and domestic duties, she did so lifelessly, with her mind on higher things. She had borne him two sons, but never showed the slightest delight in sexual relations, which had been infrequent and short-lived, nor, he suspected, in her maternal bond with her children. Above all, she had never adapted to life in Madrid, and really tried to recreate there the habits and customs of her mother's home in the country. She was a latter-day mystic, who lived out her daily contacts with other human beings in a perfunctory manner.

When they reached their ancient apartment on the top floor of the building, she tut-tutted at the dust her husband and son had allowed to accumulate, and looked in resignation at the pile of dirty plates in the kitchen.

'I'll clear this up and make some supper soon, Luis, but I'll just say a short prayer.'

She at once disappeared into a large cupboard off the dining-room, where Luis could hear her connecting the plug for the electric candles and coloured lights that decorated a half-lifesize statue of Our Lady of the Sorrows, to which she was wont to pray at regular intervals.

ATOCHA

On Tuesday, 31 May, Bernal received an urgent call from the DGS at 8.10 a.m. Inspector Martín of Retiro District would like him to go at once to Atocha Metro station. Bernal rang his office and left a message for Navarro to meet him there. With a feeling of excitement and foreboding, he told Eugenia that he didn't have time to take breakfast, which anyway consisted as usual of stale bread fried in olive oil and an *ersatz* coffee made of chicory and acorns. He was lucky to find a taxi just being vacated outside the Church of San Manuel and San Benito.

As the taxi crawled in the morning rush around the Plaza de la Independencia and down the Calle de Alfonso XII, Bernal again pondered on the facts which had so far emerged in the Metro case. It was now clear that the same person was responsible for the two dummies being left in the trains, because Varga the technician had rung him the night before to tell him that the blood contained in small plastic bags and forced into the mouths of the dummies and the murdered girl was all B negative, and the three samples matched exactly in the MN and Hr factors. Thus it had all come from the same person, almost a litre and a half of it, and it couldn't have been taken from the veins of the girl, who had been killed after the dummies had been left, and who had a different blood group anyway—O positive.

Whose blood was it? That was what intrigued him. It wasn't likely that it had come from a blood bank, first because it wasn't diluted with extra plasma, and secondly, because it was not normal for the same donor to give more than a litre on any one occasion. Yet the 'blood print' showed that it had all come from the same person, a healthy young adult who had antibodies against the usual diseases of childhood and adolescence. Bernal began more and more to sense that he was up against a maniacal multiple murderer. What could his purpose be, even within the terms of his own psychopathy, in leaving the corpse and the dummies in the Underground? Presumably to cause public alarm, but was there more to it than that? Could the perpetrator have some perverted fantasy about corpses in the Metro which were bleeding from the mouth?

Bernal asked the taxi-driver to take a short-cut down the Callejón del Doctor Velasco alongside the Ministry of Agriculture, and to leave him at the lower corner, opposite Atocha Railway station. He walked past the old woman who sold peanuts and sweets wrapped in brightly coloured papers, and who was just beginning to spread out her wares on a small trestle table, and the blind lottery-ticket seller, who was pegging up his strips of tickets in the window of his kiosk. As Bernal came up to the Metro entrance, he saw two grey-uniformed policemen who were preventing indignant travellers from entering the station. Bernal showed them his warrant card and hurried down the steps into the hallway where the pleasant-looking *taquillera* stood white-faced at the door of her ticket-office.

'There's a dead woman down there,' she said, 'on the down-line platform.'

'I'm Superintendent Bernal. Which platform is that?'

'Straight on when you go through the barrier, direction Portazgo.'

Bernal glanced at the walls which were plastered with political posters, mainly left-wing ones in this working-class district, and was momentarily arrested by a large *graffito*, sprayed on with red paint, which read, '*Los obreros estamos hasta los cojones de que nos suban los precios*—We workers are fed up to the balls with the rising prices.'

At the foot of the steps that led to the platform, Inspector Martín was waiting for him. 'There's been quite a lot of panic on the train, Superintendent. And the passengers messed things up for us. The corpse of a girl was discovered on a southbound train before it arrived at this station, and the women in the carriage started screaming their heads off at the blood pouring from her mouth. When the train stopped, they scrambled for the doors. A workman, who had lifted the fallen corpse, carried it out to the platform and then went to fetch the station-master. Of course, in the meantime, the doors closed and the train pulled out. The station-master rang the next station, Menéndez Pelayo, and had the train halted there. It was taken out of service and is now at the terminus at Portazgo. I called in some of my uniformed men to control the crowds on the platform and keep them to the mainline station end. We've closed this entrance, as you'll have seen.'

'We had a very similar homicide three days ago, Martín, at Tirso de Molina station. Inspector Arévalo called us in. Have you rung for Dr Peláez?'

'He's on his way, as well as the duty judge. We'll need his permission to move the body.'

'It's a pity the workman moved the body. Is he still here?'

'Yes, I've held him in the station-master's office for questioning.'

Peláez now arrived, his inquisitive eyes sparkling and absurdly magnified by his thick pebble lenses. 'Another one, Luis! And on my doorstep, too. We hardly need an ambulance. The attendants could carry her out at the other end of the platform and up the Calle de Drumen to my laboratory.' He knelt at the side of the girl and began his initial examination. 'H'm, still quite warm. Needle marks in left arm. Been injected with something.' He gently lifted the eyelids. 'Dilation of pupils just beginning to relax *post mortem* — barbiturates, amphetamine or cocaine, probably. I'll have to send specimens of the blood, tissues and organs to the toxicologist.' He took out a thermometer and checked the temperature under the left armpit. 'Not really satisfactory, Luis, but it's a bit public here to insert it in the rectum. Still, we'll have a rough idea. H'm, only been dead for an hour or so. No obvious marks of violence. I'll have a closer look later.' He took a pair of tweezers from his bag and pushed them through the bloodstained lips and teeth. 'Ha! Thought so! A plastic bag like before. This blood's not come out of her, Luis. Strange trick to play, isn't it?'

The judge of instruction who was on duty arrived, and after discussing the case with Bernal, Martín and Peláez, authorized the removal of the cadaver to the Instituto Anatómico Forense in the Calle de Santa Isabel nearby. Martín tugged at Bernal's sleeve and pointed to two figures approaching along the platform.

'They're newspapermen, Superintendent. How have they heard so quickly?'

Bernal greeted one of the reporters, whom he knew by sight.

'How did you hear about this?'

'An anonymous phone call half an hour ago, Superintendent. A man with a gruff voice, the telephonist said. What's up?'

'A corpse of a girl was found on a train,' said Bernal.

'Lots of blood, isn't there? Can my photographer here take some shots?'

Bernal considered the wisdom of this. 'Well, be quick, then. We're going to move the body to the lab shortly.' If the press had been tipped off anonymously, perhaps by the murderer, he thought it would be useless, in the new political climate, to try and stop them printing the news. But he decided against volunteering any information about the earlier case or about the dummies, not to let them blow it up into a sensational crime. Perhaps that was what the murderer wanted.

'A pretty girl she must have been,' said the reporter. 'In her twenties, wouldn't you say? Her hair looks dyed blonde.' He looked in pity at the small figure in the crumpled red dress. 'I wonder what she did to deserve this? How did she die? Was she stabbed?' He pointed at the blood staining the clothes and part of the platform.

'We're not sure yet,' said Bernal, turning his head away from the sight. 'Dr Peláez will be doing the autopsy shortly.'

The stark white flashes from the news-photographer's camera added an eeriness to the scene, and the passengers herded by three policemen to the further end of the platform looked on in stunned fascination.

Inspector Navarro now came on the scene, accompanied by the police photographer. The latter glared with professional rage at the newspaper men who had beaten him to it, and took the official photographs for the judge. Then the sad procession of attendants, pathologist, judge and reporters set off towards the far exit through the silent commuters. The station staff threw sand on the bloodstains, and the service on Line 1 was resumed.

'I want to have a chat with you and Navarro,' Bernal said quietly to Martín. 'Let's go up and have a coffee. I haven't breakfasted yet.'

In the cool morning air they strolled along the Paseo de la Infanta Isabel, and went into the bar of the Hotel Sur, where they ensconced themselves comfortably at a corner table and gazed at the enormous array of fresh breakfast pastries: hot *churros* and *porras, palmeras, españolas, lazos, brioches, torteles, suizos* and many more.

'I've a feeling we're confronted by a maniacal mass-murderer,' Bernal began gravely, 'but I don't want the public to be panicked.' He gave Martín a brief account of the dummies, the first girl to be murdered, and the characteristic plastic bag of blood in the mouth in each case. 'I didn't think it wise to try and stop the press from reporting this morning's case, but we must keep quiet about the earlier incidents. I'll have a chat with the director of the Metropolitan Company later. I'm sure they won't want their passengers alarmed. The most urgent task is to identify the dead girls.'

'Shouldn't we go to Portazgo to look at the coach where the last girl was found?' asked Navarro.

'I was hoping you and Martín would do that, Paco. See if she had a handbag or anything to identify her by. Varga will have a look at the clothes later, when Peláez sends them up to us.'

SOL

At 1 p.m. the same day, Peláez rang Bernal. 'I've cut her open, Luis, and there are clear signs that she was suffocated, probably while drugged with an alkaloid. There's no sign of sexual molestation. She wasn't a virgin, and there's some disturbance in the womb — some scarring. Well cared for. Upper middle-class, I'd say, by the state of the hands and the careful use of cosmetics. Killed early this morning, say between 5 and 7 a.m.'

'Well, that didn't leave the murderer much time to get the body down to the Metro, if that's what he did. Was the drug injected?' asked Bernal.

'Most probably. Needle-marks in the left arm, you'll recall. I've sent the organs over to Toxicology. They'll work out the approximate dosage from the blood, liver, and brain tissue. She hadn't eaten for over six hours. Nothing in the stomach. I assume you want me to send her fingerprints over with my preliminary report.'

'Thank you, Peláez. I hope we don't get any more of these.'

'Oh, I think you will, unless you can get to him straightaway.'

After he had rung off, Bernal looked at the large map of the Metro system which now adorned one wall of his office. Cuatro Caminos station was the key, he was sure. Only Lines 1 and 2 had been involved so far, and although in the latest case they had no idea how long the murdered girl had been in the carriage, the train had certainly stopped at Cuatro Caminos en route. He called Navarro in.

'I want to put a full surveillance on Cuatro Caminos station. Get Ángel to organize it with Elena. They can take turns there with some armed plainclothesmen, who had better be disguised as Metro staff. I'll ring the director and get his cooperation. After all, it's quite a common thing to see company employees chatting to a ticket-clerk in her office, and Elena and Ángel know what to look for.'

'I'll see to it, *jefe*.'

'I've had another thought,' said Bernal. 'What if it's a disgruntled ex-employee of the company?'

'A rather exaggerated way to go about it, chief. What about one of the private shareholders? They haven't had a dividend this year.'

'I think that's even less likely. But just in case, could you go round to the headquarters and see their personnel director? He could give us a list of employees recently dismissed for any reason. When I ring the Company director, I'll see if they've had any threats from shareholders or anyone else.'

RETIRO

After his discussion by telephone with the Metro director, which was uninformative, Bernal went home to lunch. As he entered the flat, Eugenia pounced on him accusingly from the terrace door.

'You didn't water the plants when I was away, Luis. Just look at this poor plant, which was the pride of my collection.' She was cleaning the drooping leaves of a *ficus elastica* with a grubby sponge.

'But it rained on two days, Geñita,' he said pacifyingly. 'I didn't think they needed watering.'

'But it was under the eaves, Luis, to keep it out of the wind. I think you've let it die. And this variegated agave, what did you do to it?'

'Nothing, Geñita. I haven't even been out on to the terrace.'

'There you are then, you see what your neglect has done?' she said with something approaching triumph. 'All my efforts to brighten up this dump are ruined.'

'Why don't we move to one of those new apartments across the park, Geñita?' They had had a running battle on this point for over five years.

'You want me to live in one of those jerry-built blocks, where I don't know anyone, with miles to go to the nearest church? All because of a plant?' She stormed into the kitchen on this unanswerable point of feminine logic, which left Luis as baffled as usual.

After lunching on rather yellowish, stringy runner-beans, which had been cooked in rancid olive-oil, Luis declined her offer of a piece of cracked Manchegan cheese, and said he had to be getting back to work.

But out in the street he took a taxi and asked the driver to take him to the Calle de Barceló.

CUATRO CAMINOS

Inspectora Elena Fernández was pent up with excitement. She had only been in Superintendent Bernal's team for two months, she was the first and only woman detective-inspector in the DGS, and now she had been asked to organize the surveillance on Cuatro Caminos station to spot the Metro murderer. It was true, of course, that she was only organizing it in conjunction with Ángel Gallardo. Her feelings towards him were mixed: when she joined the group, he had been pointed out to her as the playboy member of it, and she knew he did undercover work in the night spots of the capital. And there was a class difference between them: she was the daughter of a rich building contractor and had been to the University and the Police School, whereas he was from a working-class family and had entered the police service young.

But it was not this that caused the strain between them; she recognized that the root of the problem was his bouncing sexuality, which never let up. He was the traditional gallant, the tireless Don Juan, who could never treat her as a colleague first and then as a woman. She was a walking challenge to his *machismo*, yet she had tried to make it clear from the outset that theirs would never be other than a working relationship. She was, after all, experienced with men, she had had a series of boyfriends, and had known how to handle this type of amatory advance since her adolescence. Nevertheless he could get under her defences simply because he exploited their professional contact. Still, he was fun to be with most of the time, was full of high spirits, and in an unassuming way he was teaching her a lot about police work.

She and Ángel met the four plainclothesmen assigned to the surveillance, and they arranged to be fitted out with Metro Company uniforms. She was given a grey smock, and Ángel a station-master's dark blue uniform. They also organized a schedule of times from 6.30 a.m. when the station opened, to 1.30 a.m. when it closed.

Ángel addressed them before they set out: 'We haven't

much to go on, but we must watch out for anyone helping
or carrying a disabled person. It's hard to guess how the
murderer managed to carry a body weighing over 40 kilos
down a flight of steps, past the ticket-clerk, through the
barrier and down to the platform without being spotted.
But we must assume that it looked normal and natural to
anyone watching.'

'What do we do if we spot someone suspicious,
Inspector?' asked the eldest of the plainclothesmen.

'Report it to Inspectora Fernández or to me — one of us
will be in the ticket-office with the *taquillera* — and then
two of you follow the suspect on to the train. Should he
leave his seemingly crippled companion, stop him and
challenge him. Check his identity *carnet*, and examine
that of his companion, and his or her state of health, of
course. Don't go leaving a corpse on the train! Then take
the suspect in for questioning to the Gobernación.'

'Have we any description to go on?' asked another of
the plainclothesmen.

'Very little. A burly man, who may be bearded, may be
not. Probably he disguises himself.'

At Cuatro Caminos, Elena greeted the *taquillera*,
whom she had interviewed earlier, and explained about
the surveillance operation, while Ángel went down to talk
to the station-master. Victoria Álvarez made Elena as
welcome as she could, and cleared a small stool for her in
the corner of the ticket-office, from where she would have
a good view of the people entering the station.

One of the plainclothesmen stationed himself opposite
the ticket office, in a doorway leading to the technicians'
store, while his companion set out coffee-making equipment inside. More experienced than Elena, they settled
down to a long wait.

TRIBUNAL

In the Calle de Barceló, the taxi drew up outside the Cafetería Pablos, and Bernal went in for a *café cortado* and a glass of Carlos III brandy, his usual after-lunch drink. Then he made for his secret apartment along the street near the Teatro Barceló.

He had bought this *pied-à-terre* three years earlier, unbeknown to his family. At first he had gone there alone in the afternoons and at weekends to relax by listening to recordings of operas on the Hitachi hi-fi system he had indulged in; his taste ran to the Italians, Verdi, Donizetti and Bellini, and to a few French composers, especially Massenet.

Then one day he had fallen in love, for the first time in his life, he realized, with Consuelo Lozano, whom he had met at the bank where she worked. She was twenty-nine years his junior, and was still a virgin when they met, and for a year thereafter. Although she had a sharp mind, she was extremely shy and frightened of men, and lived a spinsterish existence looking after her invalid mother. But a rapport had sprung up at once between the banker's secretary and the senior detective, who was old enough to be her father. He had taken her out, and given her small gifts, which had embarrassed her. But she was warm and loving by nature, and on the third occasion he had taken her to the secret apartment he had made love to her, very gently, for the first time, and had awakened her natural passion; this had made her bloom with self-confidence. During the past two years she had given him more fulfilment than Eugenia had in forty years of marriage.

He felt no sense of guilt, other than the legal guilt the Spanish penal code placed on adulterers, by which the woman involved was liable to up to six months' imprisonment. They never talked of the future, just as he and Eugenia had never spoken of it. Both the women in his

life behaved as though their respective situations were
eternal.

There had been no divorce law since the end of the
Civil War, and the possibility of applying to the Vatican
for an annulment was a remote one. What could the
grounds be? He realized how difficult it would be to
confess his infidelity to Eugenia, or to broach the question
of separation. He didn't think it would now matter much
to his children: his elder son was married with a son of his
own, and Diego the younger son was grown up and
studying at the University. Nor was it the embarrassment
in his professional life that held him back. It was simply
that it would be the worst sort of betrayal in Eugenia's
eyes; her life would crumble into uncomprehended ruins.
If he felt nothing else for her, there was still a kind of
loyalty, the remnant of long habit.

He found Consuelo in the kitchen of his apartment,
making herself a *bocadillo* — a small Vienna loaf cut in
half, which she was filling with salad and fresh white
Manchegan cheese.

'Luchi, what kept you so late?'

'It's been a difficult morning, love.' He embraced her,
and gave her an account of the dead girl found at Atocha
and the similarities with the corpse found earlier at
Ventas.

'And you can't identify either of the murdered girls?'

'I've only just sent the fingerprints of the second corpse
to the DNI, and it could take them weeks to track her
down in the national files.'

'But why should the murderer take the considerable
risk of taking the bodies into the Metro?'

'To cause panic, I think, love. That's why he puts the
plastic bags full of blood into the mouths.'

'You don't think he stays to watch his handiwork when
the body is discovered, Luchi? To get a sort of thrill?'

'I hadn't thought of that.' Bernal reflected on the

earlier incidents. 'He couldn't have done so with the first body, because it was found late at night, and there was only one woman and three lads in the carriage at the time.'

They chatted a little more, since Bernal found she helped to clarify his thoughts with her direct questions and practical banker's mind. After a while, slowly and naturally, they began to undress and move towards the bedroom.

SOL

The next day Bernal's team had a piece of luck. Missing Persons had rung to say that a Señora Ledesma had reported her daughter missing for eleven days. The description might fit the girl found dead at Tirso de Molina station. Bernal asked them to send the woman to his office, and he called Elena in. She was being temporarily relieved by Ángel from the watch they were keeping at Cuatro Caminos station, which had proved fruitless so far.

Señora Ledesma entered nervously, obviously alarmed at being in a police station, let alone the headquarters of the Dirección General de Seguridad. Despite a clear lack of wealth, she was neatly dressed in a worn but tailored brown coat, and sat nervously twisting a thin wedding ring round the fourth finger of her right hand.

'Where does your daughter work, señora?' Bernal asked in a kindly manner.

'She works for a typing agency, and gets sent out to different jobs each week or fortnight.'

'Does she live with you?'

'She used to, but six months ago she began renting a one-roomed studio apartment in El Carmen quarter.'

'How long is it since you've seen her, señora?'

'We only see her on Sundays now. She doesn't get on with her father, you see. He's always on to her about her painting her fingernails, or dyeing her hair blonde; neither does he like the man she goes out with. That's why she moved out. I usually meet her on a Saturday afternoon, without her father knowing, and we go shopping together. But she didn't turn up this weekend.' She twisted a handkerchief between her fingers, and looked unhappily at Bernal.

Elena asked her, 'What's your daughter's full name, señora?'

'Paloma Ledesma Pascual.'

'Did she have a steady boy-friend?'

'No, not really. She did some years ago, when she was younger. She's twenty-two now, and I'd like her to get married. I keep telling her she'll get left on the shelf, but she will go out with these older men, men she works for sometimes, when the agency sends her out.'

'I see,' said Bernal. 'Does she have any outside interests or hobbies?'

'Not until all this politicking began. She joined the Popular Socialist Party and goes round to help them with typing out the election propaganda in the evenings. Her father doesn't mind that. He's been a lifelong socialist,' she said, raising her head defiantly, as though she was now free to say something she couldn't have said, not in those premises anyway, for the past thirty-eight years.

'Señora Ledesma, I take it you've been to your daughter's apartment?'

'Yes, I have. She lets me keep a key, so that I can go in to clean it for her when she's at work.'

'And you didn't find any clue as to where she might have gone?' persisted Bernal.

'No, there's nothing missing, except the clothes she must have been wearing, and no note, or anything like that.'

'Will you be able to give us a description of the clothes?'

'Yes, of course, but I've already given a list to Missing Persons.'

'Good, good,' said Bernal cheerfully. 'I'm sure your daughter is somewhere safe and sound, perhaps with friends, but since you haven't heard from her for eleven days, nor has the porter of the building where she lives seen her, I—' Bernal hesitated—'I should like you to help us. There's an unknown girl we can't identify, who could possibly fit your daughter's description.'

'You mean she's dead, don't you, this girl you want me to look at? I can't do it, I won't.' She broke down, and Elena went to her side.

'Don't worry,' said Elena, 'you don't have to. Perhaps your husband . . . ?'

'No, no, I'll spare him that,' she said vehemently. 'I'll go with you. Let's get it over with.'

ATOCHA

Señora Ledesma was silent as the three of them were driven down to the Calle de Santa Isabel. Dr Peláez met them, and showed them into a waiting-room. He took Bernal aside.

'We've cleaned her up, Luis, and she doesn't look too bad. You can bring the woman in now.'

The mother blenched as the refrigerator drawer was pulled open, and gave a muffled scream and fainted into Bernal's arms as she recognized her daughter.

SOL

Bernal now galvanized his team into action. They obtained lists of Paloma Ledesma's recent employers from the typing agency, and set off to interview them. Navarro was sent to the party headquarters of the PSP, where Paloma had been a volunteer worker. Her mother failed to recognize the clothes found on her daughter's corpse, and was sure they weren't hers, apart from the red scarf. She also said that a large ring set with an amethyst was missing from her daughter's left hand.

The small studio flat Paloma had rented in El Carmen was thoroughly searched, and all the surfaces were tested for latent prints, with no positive results, except for the prints of the dead girl. Varga even examined the sumps of the washbasin and bath for hairs, but they all proved to be similar to hers. The only discovery they made was a small amount of cocaine in a white envelope. Clearly she had been a cocaine-sniffer. Bernal wondered who among her men friends had introduced her to that.

It took them three days to complete the interviews with her former employers and the PSP party workers who knew her, and the inquiry got no further ahead. All those questioned were checked in the criminal files, but nothing of importance was known about any of them. The surveillance at Cuatro Caminos Metro station still produced no result.

In the meantime Bernal received the final reports on the second murdered girl, who had still not been identified. Her blood group was AB positive, thus differing from the B negative blood that had oozed from the plastic sac found in her mouth. She had been injected, or had injected herself, with cocaine, and had been asphyxiated, but not by manual strangulation, while unconscious. Photographs of her were shown to the Ledesmas, and to Paloma's employers and acquaintances, but none claimed to recognize the unknown girl. Yet Bernal felt that the two girls might have been acquainted, perhaps in some bar or night-club where they used to go, except that Paloma Ledesma appeared to have led no social life to speak of, according to those who had known her, or at least, none would reveal it.

He managed to master his initial feeling of being balked; after all, someone must know something, but for the moment it was difficult to tell who was deliberately keeping quiet. If only the second girl could be identified, then he could look for a connection between the victims, which might show up a pattern in the killings and lead him to the murderer. One plus one was worth much more than two.

He looked down at the crush of people in the brightly lit Calle de Carretas below the window of his office. The shops had closed at 7.30 p.m., but the number of window-shoppers, waiting sweethearts, bar-crawlers and hustlers of both sexes had not decreased. It was the hour to take *tapas* or pre-dinner snacks, washed down with *cañas* of beer or *chatos* of white wine. A few yards down the street, where it joined the Puerta del Sol, the social hub of the city, he could just glimpse a line of cars whose occupants were waving the national flag out of the windows and blowing their horns in a syncopated rhythm. Falangists? Or Fuerza Nueva? Certainly a right-wing group protesting at the legalization of the Communist Party. He had read in the night reports that there had been minor skirmishes between rival groups in the Gran Vía and in the Plaza de Callao for three successive nights. The Minister had asked the Antidisturbios squads to stand by at key points.

Locking the office, Bernal made his way to the side exit, and was immediately swallowed up by the evening *paseo*, but he managed to buy an evening paper. The headlines alarmed him: PANIC IN THE METRO! GIRL MURDERED ON TRAIN AT ATOCHA! The press had not lost interest in the affair. This issue contained a quite uninformed account of the second murder, mainly derived from exaggerated stories provided by the female witnesses whom the reporters had tracked down. But these were overshadowed by an eye-riveting blown-up photograph of the blood-stained corpse on the edge of the platform at Atocha Metro station. As he descended the steps of the Underground, Bernal sensed that the murderer, somewhere, at that moment, was gloating over the sensational report.

VELÁZQUEZ

That night at the headquarters of the PSOE, the Workers' Socialist Party, there was feverish activity in readiness for the many open-air meetings and rallies planned for the last run-up to the General Election. The girls who were helping to sew the party's initials in gold on the red banners were chatting excitedly. Would the leader, Felipe González, come in tonight to add his encouragement?

'I'll swoon if he comes to talk to me!' Isabel Ordóñez confided to the girl next to her. 'He's so virile, so magnetic.'

'He's got a pretty wife, too,' said her companion mischievously. 'By the way, I wonder what's happened to that other girl, Mari Luz? This is the fifth night she's missed.'

'Perhaps her new boy-friend is taking her out,' replied Isabel. 'He looked a bit old for her, in his forties, I'd say. I saw him waiting outside for her, a week ago it was. Odd-looking fellow—quite tall but stoutish, with a gaunt face. There was a strange, intense look in his eyes as he watched us coming down the front steps. He looked better when he smiled.'

LISTA

At 9 a.m. precisely on Friday, 3 June, in the Calle del Conde de Peñalver, the prim manager of the Peñalver bookshop was dictating a letter to be sent to María Luz Cabrera Salazar.

'Never,' he exclaimed to his middle-aged, bespectacled secretary, 'never in twenty years have I had an employee stay away from work without explanation like this! Almost a whole week! And a good employee too.' The secretary pursed her lips. 'Yes, I know she's a bit flighty and chats up the male customers, but that's good for business. And she knows where the books are. But she'll have to go, she really will. And from such a good family. Her father a lieutenant-general, and a friend of the proprietor.'

'Shouldn't we perhaps ring up the family to see if she's ill?' asked the secretary tentatively.

'Well, you know she lives alone in a flat in Quevedo, and I tried ringing her there all last week without success.'

'But her family home? Wouldn't it be safer to ring her father before sending the letter? I mean, if he's a friend of the proprietor . . .'

'Yes, perhaps you're right. Would you look up the number for me?'

Mari Luz's father the lieutenant-general was appalled to hear of his daughter's truancy from work. He would contact her at once, despite their recent differences over politics.

QUEVEDO

As he was driven in the official car to his daughter's studio flat, General Cabrera asked himself how he could possibly have produced a communist child. For that's what she was, he had told her repeatedly, whatever her party called itself. All of them, he insisted, were run by marxists and freemasons, just as the late Generalísimo had forecast, and they would bring Spain to ruination.

He strode into the modern apartment block in the Calle de Eloy Gonzalo, ignoring the porter, and took the lift to his daughter's flat. After hammering in vain for a few minutes, he descended in the lift to question the desk-clerk. This nervous young man was made to reveal that Mari Luz had not been in for almost a week, and he was inveigled into producing a duplicate key. He retained sufficient nerve to insist on accompanying the old martinet on his inspection of the studio.

The general stumped around the room, aimlessly picking up and putting down ornaments, which were all either of stainless steel or chunky Swedish glass. He gazed at the modern and slightly surrealist décor in obvious distaste. 'Why can't she stay at home and live with her family like any decent, God-fearing girl, eh?' He addressed the young desk-clerk, but obviously did not expect a reply. 'Well, there's no help for it. I'm going to ring Missing Persons.' He marched purposefully towards the telephone. 'Did you see her leave with anyone?' he demanded of the desk-clerk.

'No . . . no, sir,' he stuttered. 'She went out at about 8 p.m. last Monday and I haven't seen her since. Shall I ask the night-porter, sir?'

'No need. The police will do all that.'

SOL

The inspector in charge of the Missing Persons Office rang Bernal with some trepidation. 'A lieutenant-general called Cabrera has just been inquiring, Superintendent, about his daughter, who hasn't been seen since the night of 30 May. The description he has given could fit the girl you found dead on the Metro on the 31st.'

'Did you tell him so?'

'No, no, I thought I'd leave you to do that. Considering his rank, sir, I wonder whether you could go to visit him in his office?'

'And where is that?' asked Bernal.

'In the Ministry of War, in the Calle de Prim.'

'Very well. I'll get Navarro to ring for an appointment and we'll call to see him.'

Navarro arranged the meeting for noon, and Bernal suggested they went in the largest of the official cars, a Seat limousine, so as to impress the military.

BANCO

General Cabrera treated them with affable condescension, though Bernal was not unaware that his own rank of Comisario de Primera was equal to the lieutenant-general's.

'I wonder if you chaps could help to find my daughter, María Luz. I haven't told the lady wife yet; she'd be distraught, don't you know. Luz is the youngest of our five children, and the only one who hasn't married and settled down. I found her a nice little job in a bookshop, owned by a friend of mine.'

'Where is the shop, General?' asked Bernal courteously.

'In the Calle de Peñalver. It's called the Librería Peñalver, I think. When she told us six months ago she wanted to live in a flat on her own, her mother was naturally upset. Since the other children left home, we moved out to a new apartment in Arturo Soria, which is still much too big for us, but the lady wife is always wanting to entertain, don't you know, so I give in to her little whims.'

'Does your daughter have a *novio* or boy-friend, General?'

'Not that I know of. She used to bring the most unsuitable young men home to meet us, but I soon put paid to them. Gold-diggers, I reckoned. Not one of them had two pesetas to rub together. I've been very worried about her recently, with all this political nonsense coming up.' The General hesitated. 'I found out she'd joined the Workers' Socialist Party. Can you imagine it, Superintendent? Dash it all, a general's daughter, with that riffraff! Even helping out at their headquarters. We quarrelled over it, and I accused her of doing it to harm the family, don't you know. Perhaps I went too far, eh? But I had a duty to warn her about the reds infiltrating these new parties, didn't I, what?' He glowered at them with an air of self-justification.

Bernal kept his expression noncommittal. 'How long has she been helping at the party headquarters, General?'

'Oh, a few weeks, I believe. Since all this damned nonsense began. She only goes there on weekday evenings, I understand.'

'Very well, we'll start our inquiries there. There is one matter you could help us with, General.' Bernal paused, and then drew out an envelope from his inside pocket. 'Would you be so kind as to look at this photograph?'

General Cabrera put on a pair of gold-rimmed half-spectacles and examined the photograph of the face of the second girl found dead on the Metro.

'Well,' he said grudgingly, 'it could be María Luz; anyway someone who looks quite like her. But this person seems very ill, Superintendent.'

'General, I'm extremely sorry to have to ask this of you, but we should like you to accompany us to make an identification.'

'You mean you've arrested my daughter?' The General exploded. 'By God, it's an outrage!'

'No, no, General, it's much worse than that. We have to ask you to look at the body of a girl in the Instituto Anatómico Forense.'

The General seemed to crumple in his chair. 'And you chaps think it's my daughter?' he managed to utter.

'We don't know. Only you will be able to tell us.'

ATOCHA

In the Calle de Santa Isabel, General Cabrera lost all his bluster and broke down when he recognized María Luz's corpse.

Bernal took him to Peláez's office, and gave him an account of the circumstances in which she had been found five days earlier at Atocha Metro station.

'You do see, General, that we may be dealing with a maniac? I need the help of your wife and yourself to make a list of your daughter's friends and acquaintances, and we shall have to examine her possessions.'

'Yes, yes, of course, Bernal,' the General murmured in a beaten tone of voice. 'Anything you say.' Then he added, 'For the family's sake, keep this out of the press, eh?'

'I'm afraid a rather sensational account has already appeared in one of the evening papers, and the reporters will follow it up if they can. We shan't, of course, issue any statement.'

'Thank you, Superintendent. You're a good chap. This news will break the lady wife.'

VELÁZQUEZ

That evening Bernal went in person to the Workers'
Socialist Party headquarters, accompanied by Navarro.
One of the organizers located the girls with whom María
Luz Cabrera had worked, and provided a room for
interviewing them.

The first two girls said they didn't know her well, and
found her pleasant but stand-offish. The third girl, Isabel
Ordóñez, had clearly got to know her better, and had
some important information for them.

'Almost a week ago, I think it was, Superintendent. We
both got ready to go home about 9.30, and outside on
the steps a man in his forties was waiting for her.'

'Can you remember the date exactly, señorita?' asked
Bernal.

'Well, it was the last night Mari Luz turned up here.
I'm pretty sure it was last Monday, five nights ago. But
the organizer will remember, I'm sure.' Bernal reflected
that that was the night before María Luz had been found
dead in the Metro. Perhaps this girl was the last person to
see her alive, apart from the murderer.

'Can you remember what this man looked like?'

'He was dressed in a dark blue suit with a striped tie. As
I said, he looked to be in his forties, with a lot of dark
hair, but clean-shaven. What struck me most was, despite
the fact he was burly, almost stout in girth, he had gaunt
cheeks. I didn't like his staring eyes.' She gave a little
shudder.

'Did you form the impression from the way Mari Luz
greeted him that it was an arranged meeting, or a casual
one?' asked Bernal.

'Oh, it definitely seemed that she was expecting him,
that it was a *cita*, an appointment.'

'Did she call him by name?'

'No, she just said "*Hola*" and shook his hand.'

'Did you see which way they went? Did they get into a car?'

'No, they walked up the street, and I turned the opposite way to catch the Metro from Velázquez.'

'Have you ever seen him apart from that one occasion? Did he ever come into these headquarters, for example?'

'Not that I know of. I never saw him before or since.'

RETIRO

The next morning Bernal was wakened at 7.30 by an icy blast blowing through the half-open bedroom door. Eugenia was up and about, and had opened the metal-lined door that led to the terrace. He got up grumpily and reached for his woollen dressing-gown. On his way through the corridor, he peered sleepily through the window-grille and spotted Eugenia out in the dawn breeze, muttering as she re-tied the *ficus elastica* to a cane. The plant looked more moribund than ever. In the kitchen he attempted to ignite the ancient gas geyser, and after applying four lighted matches, jumped back towards the door as a muffled explosion lifted the rusty cover of the contraption clean into the air. It fell with a clang into the sink, just missing the coffee pot which gurgled on the stove.

In the bathroom Bernal thought he had managed to steal a march on the insurance agent who lived immediately below, because so far no foul smells had gurgled up the drainpipes. Oh God, how he hated this awful apartment, where nothing ever worked.

After dressing in one of his better suits and tying a silk tie his younger son had bought in the Corte Inglés, the big department store, for his birthday, he told Eugenia that an official car was meeting him shortly to take him to the general's house. Eugenia was interested in the visit, since she naturally approved of the generals appointed by Franco. She was shocked when he told her of the daughter's murder.

'And in the Metro! And at Atocha too! What an unsuitable place to be found dead in! Had the girl gone off the rails, Luis?' Since her theological discussions with the parish priest led her to believe in a somewhat strict view of providential cause and effect, based on a literal interpretation of the text 'The wages of sin is death,' she could not accept that any person in a state of grace could get murdered.

Assuming she had not intended a macabre word-play in her last remark, Luis replied, 'Not that I know of, Geñita, but she had recently become a *militante* in the Workers' Socialist Party.'

'There you are, then! That explains it! Got mixed up with the reds or the anarchists. Silly little girl, trying to show up her parents like that. No wonder she got killed! These political parties will be the ruin of Spain, Luis, you mark my words!'

Bernal left most of the artificial coffee and the fried stale bread, claiming that the car would be waiting. Once out in the Calle de Alcalá, he took another and better breakfast in Félix Pérez's bar, keeping an eye open for the car which Navarro was bringing.

CIUDAD LINEAL

As their driver negotiated the thick commuter traffic coming into the city from the east, Bernal discussed the Metro case with Navarro, offering him a Kaiser from a crumpled packet.

'Do you think the motive is political, *jefe*?' asked

Navarro. 'Both the girls worked in the headquarters of the two principal socialist parties.'

'You mean as a warning, or to hit out at the Left? And then he goes to the bother of carting the bodies down to the Underground? I see the point that the press could sensationalize the affair: "Political murders in the Metro!" It might frighten the other girls who are helping the left-wing parties. But what about the dummies? There was nothing political about them.'

'Perhaps he hoped to have a whole press sensation going by now, but it hasn't worked out the way he wanted.'

'In that case,' said Bernal, 'I should have expected him to tip off the press about the dummies and the first murder, but he hasn't done so yet, apparently. It's true the reporters who turned up at Atocha got a tip-off, but there was time for one of the passengers on the train to phone them anonymously.'

'Is it to do with drugs, then, chief? The first girl, Paloma Ledesma, sniffed cocaine, and María Luz Cabrera had been injected with some kind of drug before she died.'

'We'll see what Varga finds in Mari Luz's apartment,' said Bernal. 'But why should anyone kill them just for being drug-addicts?'

'To stop them talking, or to punish them?'

'In that case, why the Metro for disposing of the bodies?'

'Less chance of detection, perhaps he thinks? And he's right so far.'

They passed the Cross of the Fallen near Ciudad Lineal Metro station, and turned left into Arturo Soria, into a much more elegant suburb. Named after Madrid's chief urban planner of the 'thirties, the avenue had a pleasant belt of trees and shrubs along the central reservation, and was edged with roomy mansions and occasional small estates of luxury flats.

The general's apartment had a private lift from the underground car-park and a fine balcony overlooking the residents' swimming pool and gardens. The general's wife received them gravely, already dressed in deepest mourning, and led them to a huge sitting-room, which was heavily furnished in traditional Spanish style, clashing with the modernity of the architecture. After introductions had been made and condolences given, Bernal went straight to the point.

'Have you any reason to think your daughter might have been experimenting with drugs, señora?'

Señora Cabrera went pale. 'No, no reason at all, Superintendent. I think I should have noticed if she were when she was still living with us.'

'Well, she had been injected with a drug shortly before her death. Did she have any men friends recently?'

'She had a large circle of friends, and sometimes held parties for them, although her father did not altogether approve and would shut himself up in his study for the evening. Some of them were rather arty, you know. But I never saw any sign of drug-taking among them.'

'Could we see her room, señora? She still kept some of her things here?'

'Oh yes, she usually came over at weekends.' Her composure showed signs of breaking. 'I'll show you the way, Superintendent.'

'Most kind. Perhaps in the meantime you could make us a list of her friends?'

The search of Mari Luz's room was fruitless. There wasn't even an address book or list of telephone numbers.

'She must have kept all her personal papers at her new apartment, Paco.'

'Clean as a whistle here, *jefe*.'

SOL

In the late afternoon of Monday, 6 June, Bernal sat on the corner of his desk, animatedly discussing the murders with Navarro.

'So far we've got no real lead, Paco. There's no apparent connection between Paloma Ledesma and María Luz Cabrera except their involvement in left-wing politics, and even then they were in different parties. Unless there's something else that connects them which we haven't yet spotted. Socially, they were as different as chalk and cheese. It hardly seems likely that they would even frequent the same restaurants, cafés or discothèques.'

'Perhaps it was the drug habit, chief,' said Paco thoughtfully. 'One was a cocaine-sniffer, apparently, and the other was certainly injected with it. Could they have used the same pusher?'

'We'd better follow that line of inquiry for the moment,' said Bernal after some reflection. 'Ask Superintendent Tomás of Estupefacientes to look into it. But we know already that neither of the girls was on file. So it's going to be virtually impossible to spot the pusher.'

'But we could ask Tomás if there have been any other deaths of addicts. Perhaps of ones who failed to pay the supplier.'

'That's a bright idea, Paco. I'm beginning to think there's not much in the political angle. It smells wrong.'

ATOCHA

Dr Peláez put down his scalpel and took the telephone receiver his secretary was handing out to him.

'Morning, Luis. You realize I'm in the middle of an autopsy?'

'Sorry, Peláez,' Bernal boomed cheerfully. 'I just wanted to know if you saw any signs of regular drug-taking in Paloma Ledesma and María Luz Cabrera.'

'No, nothing really, though the first of my Metro girls, as I now think of them, had some contraction of the nasal veins. Perhaps she sniffed cocaine from time to time. I don't suppose she took snuff, eh? People don't much these days, especially not at that age.'

'Did they have any other physiological abnormality in common?'

'Not so as you'd notice. The second girl had some scarring in the Fallopian tube. She may have had an abortion. But no marks in the first cadaver, though she had had recent dental fillings. Nothing that ties up well.'

'If the first of your Metro girls had had an abortion, could it have been done so as you'd not notice at the autopsy?' asked Bernal. 'Especially if it had been done some months ago by a good gynæcologist? So many of them go to London to have it done nowadays, where it's legal and cheap. That film *Abortar en Londres* gave girls the idea, after it ran for months in the suburban cinemas.'

'If it had been done properly, some months ago, then I might not spot it, Luis. But you know the illegal back-street arrangements still go on here, often with fatal results, which automatically pass to me?'

'There may be little in the idea, Peláez, especially since the first girl had very limited means. But there's always the boy-friend . . .'

'It's only an outside chance, Luis. My feeling about the Metro girls is that you're looking for quite a young man, up to middle age, who's in an advanced psychopathic state. Let's pray he's not of the type that kill again and again, with increasing frequency until he's caught. Of course, there's another kind, who only kill when subjected to a particular stimulus which occurs fairly seldom.'

'These are the most challenging cases, Peláez, when there's no apparent connection between the killer and the victims, or between the victims, who are chosen quite arbitrarily. Let's hope our feeling about this one is wrong. After all, the motive could be a settlement of accounts by a drugs or abortion ring, or political revenge in a vague sort of way. But if it's hatred of promiscuous girls, or just girls who happen to wear red scarves, or mauve lipstick, then we're in trouble. Because we've got absolutely nothing to go on, except for Cuatro Caminos station being the probable method of ingress into the Metro system.'

'But don't forget the dolls, Luis. I think they point to a very rare and peculiar psychopath, especially the detail of the sacs of blood placed in the mouths.'

'And what if it's being done to make us think it's a psychopath's handiwork, while the real motive is to cause public panic on the eve of the General Election?'

'I suppose that's possible, but the perpetrator would really have had to mug up some criminal psychology. I'll have to ring off now, Luis. By the way, don't forget to ask yourself where the B negative blood is coming from.'

CUATRO CAMINOS

Elena was feeling tired for the first time since she had joined Bernal's team two months earlier, but the weariness was accompanied by that sense of exhilaration derived from prolonged concentration. Until now she had done all that had been asked of her with verve and super efficiency, she thought. After all, to be the first woman detective-inspector in the DGS, and still the only one not confined to the drugs group or to abortion cases, gave her a uniqueness she was determined to exploit. She guessed that her male colleagues were still wary of her, and were anxious to hide from her the more sordid aspects of their work. Well, she would show them that she had just as strong a stomach as they, perhaps stronger, since she firmly believed that women were much tougher when it came to physical unpleasantness, as mothers, nurses and nuns demonstrated every day in hospitals, asylums and in their private homes. Men, she thought, got softer as they got older, more disposed to suffer nausea at the first bad smell they came across, though she exempted from this judgement the firemen and ambulance drivers, and, of course, Dr Peláez, whom she secretly suspected of necrophilia.

After eight days spent in Cuatro Caminos station cooped up in the ticket-office with Victoria Álvarez most of the time, whose topics of conversation had proved to be quite limited, Elena began to have doubts about the validity of what they were doing there. She and Ángel Gallardo had investigated everything remotely suspicious, including the searching of beggars, cripples, and gipsy children carrying bundles of trinkets and clothes to sell in the Underground. And the result was entirely negative.

Just as she was pondering on the hopelessness of the job, Elena sensed, rather than saw, Victoria Álvarez stiffen at her side, and she looked sharply at the passengers who were in the queue to buy tickets. As a large bearded man, dressed in a beige raincoat and slouch hat drew near to the ticket window, Victoria's hands began to shake. She turned white-faced to Inspectora Fernández, who made a discreet shushing noise to try and calm her and make her behave normally. The stout man appeared to pay them no heed as he slapped down a five-duro piece and asked for one ticket, but Victoria fumbled with the change.

After he'd passed, she said to Elena, 'That's him! I'm sure of it! The one who brought a cripple down that rainy Thursday.'

Elena did not hesitate to put the emergency procedure into operation. She pressed the buzzer the technicians had installed in the ticket-office, and set out to follow the suspect down the stairs. She had to see whether he chose Line 1 or Line 2, and if Line 1 whether the platform for the northbound or southbound trains. Line 2 started from Cuatro Caminos station, so he could only go southwards on those trains. She could see her quarry stepping down the stairs quite briskly for his apparent age and weight, and she glanced nervously back to make sure the first of the plainclothesmen was following her as planned.

At the bottom of the first flight of stairs, the suspect turned to Line 1 southbound, without glancing at the indicator boards, which showed that he knew the station well, she thought. There weren't many people on the platform, so she would have to do the next bit with circumspection. Without looking at all at the suspect, who had stopped almost half way along the platform to await the train, she looked back at the first plain-clothesman who was now quite close behind her, and at the second, who had just followed them on to the platform. As she passed behind the burly, bearded man she made the pre-arranged signal with her hand to her hair to 'finger' the suspect for the others, and turned into the station-master's glass-fronted office, with her heart pounding. It was quite different doing it in real life for the first time rather than the practice runs they had done at the Police School. She hoped she hadn't acted abnormally in any way, so as to give rise to suspicion. But after all, she was dressed in the Metropolitan Company's uniform for female employees, and she wore little make-up and had her hair arranged in a workaday manner; it should look quite natural for her to go in to talk to the station-master. But when she had half-turned away and touched her hair, the bearded man's eyes were fixed on her with unusual intensity, and followed her later movements with a peculiar sharpness.

Elena sat down at the back of the glass-fronted office, feeling a little weak in the knees, and asked the Company official if she could use the phone. When she got through to Bernal's office the train was already drawing in.

'What number is this one?' she asked the station-master.

'Number thirty-three, miss.'

As a mere passenger in the past she had never noticed the small square of white cardboard bearing a number that appeared in the window of the driving-cab of each Metro train, but she now realized that the throbbing lights on the illuminated plan of the Metro Line on the wall behind her referred to those numbers and the position of each train at any given moment.

She spoke to Paco Navarro and asked him to put Inspector Miranda on the line, as Bernal had arranged. Carlos Miranda was their best shadower of suspects and he would now slip down to Sol station and take over from the two plainclothesmen.

'It's train number thirty-three on Line One, south-bound, Carlos,' she rattled out quickly. 'It's just leaving here, and he's got into the fourth carriage from the front. I don't think he's spotted me, though he keeps looking this way. He's fortyish, burly and bearded, wearing a beige mackintosh and a dark felt hat pulled over his eyes.'

ATOCHA

The changeover of police shadowers at Sol appeared to go off perfectly, without the quarry showing any sign of nervousness. Miranda looked so ordinary in his worn suit, with the sort of spectacles used by half a million *madrileños*. He got into the third carriage, from where he could see the suspect through the windows of the emergency doors at the point where the carriages were coupled.

After they left Sol, Miranda got a little nervous, because there were fewer passengers on the southerly run towards Portazgo. Many of these had the poorer, worn appearance of the working-class unemployed, and he was surprised to see how young many of them were. No doubt they had been on the daily rounds of the employers begging unsuccessfully for work. The suburb of Vallecas, where Portazgo was, and the other working-class districts were already showing the effects of the country's having over a million out of work, the rapid inflation, and the end of the industrial boom of the 'sixties.

Miranda watched carefully at Tirso de Molina and Antón Martín stations, but the burly suspect showed no signs of getting up from his seat just inside the door of the fourth carriage. As the train approached Atocha, running rapidly downhill, with the brakes squealing as the driver began to apply them, the man got to his feet and stood waiting for the doors to open. Miranda was glad it was this station, because a reasonable number of people would be getting off for the mainline station above. When the doors opened, Miranda delayed his exit from the third carriage until the last possible moment, and emerged to see the suspect walking towards the back of the train and the main exit to the RENFE station and Atocha Square. This too was a relief: it made his job much easier than if he had gone out through the Ministry of Agriculture exit, which was much less used.

In the long passenger tunnels, Miranda kept back on the opposite side of the walkway, always allowing three or four people to come between him and his quarry, until he saw which stairs he made for. Ah, not the mainline station approaches, then, but the stairs that led to the corner of the Calle de Atocha and Atocha Square, or, as it was officially named, the Glorieta del Emperador Carlos V, though no one called it such. Miranda now hurried and boldly passed the burly man on the stairs, stopping at the first kiosk to buy a newspaper as he emerged on to the street. It was getting dark and the large amber sodium lights were already warming up above the intense traffic which flowed across the square and thumped metallically on the complex flyover. This had been the first monstrosity of its kind built in Madrid in the 'sixties, and the locals had immediately christened it the 'Scalextric', not only because of its appearance but also because there happened to be an illuminated sign advertising the toy game on the roof of the houses over-looking the square.

As the burly man came up the stairs at a steady pace, Miranda glanced down at the newspaper headlines, turning half away, but watching for the direction he would take. The evening was cool, with a hint of rain, yet the *paseo* was busy at this point, with travellers passing by with luggage and parcels of all descriptions, lottery-ticket sellers vociferously proclaiming that they had the winning ticket for *el gordo* or 'the fat prize', shoeshine men wearily carrying their stools and polish-boxes, calling out '*¡Limpiar! ¡Limpiar!*' and pointing to the dirty shoes of the passers-by or those few with more time who sat at the tables of a street café watching the world go by. The suspect turned into this mêlée and Miranda moved quickly to keep close behind him. Without looking back, the bearded man entered El Brillante.

For Miranda it was quite a shock. He had never been into this *freiduría* or frying shop, which was very wide and long with a bar on each side along its full length, and a short staircase in the middle leading to a higher level. The floor near the bars was almost ankle-deep in used paper-napkins, torn-off prawn-shells, olive stones and other débris. The place was packed with people taking evening *tapas* with *cañas* of beer or *chatos* of wine, and the air sizzled with the smoke from *calamares fritos* or squids' tentacles in batter, *croquetas* of chicken and fish, prawns *a la gabardina* — in 'mackintoshes' of batter — and one was deafened by the seemingly endless shouting of orders from the barmen along both sides of the enormous eating-house: *'¡Dos de calamares! ¡Uno de patatas brava!'*

Miranda was fascinated and appalled at the same time. The suspect stopped at the nearest available free space at the bar and ordered a *caña* and a ration of fried squid, and this order was immediately and very loudly transmitted by the cheerful barman, who never ceased to wipe down the counter and sluice the dirty glasses in the zinc sink behind it. Miranda stood five customers away, pretending to choose from the list of *tapas* on the wall. Then he ordered *'un corto'*. The small glass consisting half of foam, half of lager, was slapped down in front of him, and it remained undrunk as he covertly watched the suspect's actions.

El Brillante was quite packed; there was hardly room to pass along the central way and steps. The bearded man now left his saucer of fried squid and moved slowly towards the stairs surmounted by a sign saying *'Teléfonos y Servicios'*. This posed a problem for Miranda, but one he had tackled many times before. If the suspect had gone to use the telephone, then it would be interesting to get close enough to see what number he dialled, or to listen to his end of the conversation, but such close pursuit would be sure to make him suspicious. If on the other hand he was going to the lavatory, there was no point in following him unless there was another exit, and, as far as Miranda could see, there wasn't. Nor would there be any windows at the basement level. He therefore decided to stay where he was and observe the top of the staircase, which wasn't easy given the large throng of customers.

Miranda saw a number of people go down and emerge from the basement stairs, but not the suspect. He used the interval to put on the raincoat he was carrying and to take off his spectacles, which were of plain glass in any case. These simple changes, he knew, made all the difference especially when a suspect might think he was being followed. After ten minutes had passed, he started to grow uneasy; finally he paid for his beer and descended the stairs rapidly. Both the telephones were in use, but neither of them by the bearded man. Miranda went into the men's lavatory, almost knowing in advance that he'd been outwitted. There was no sign of the suspect. Miranda emerged quickly, and hesitated at the door of the ladies'. The old female attendant who was sitting bent over her knitting in the doorway glanced up at him curiously. He showed her his police *placa* or metal badge with the yoke and arrows on it and asked her if she'd seen a large, bearded man going into the ladies'.

'Over my dead body!' she cackled.

'But did you see him pass through here?'

'So many go in and out,' she said, 'I don't try to remember them. I can assure you no man has come into the *Señoras*.'

'And there's no other way out?'

'None,' she asserted, shaking her head.

Miranda ran up the steps, through the crowded bar and out through the rear exit which led into the Calle de Drumen, looking anxiously about him in the gathering darkness. But he knew it was too late.

CUATRO CAMINOS

Elena Fernández was on tenterhooks to find out what had happened to the bearded suspect being shadowed by

Inspector Miranda. The plainclothesmen when they returned simply reported that the changeover had gone as planned. Victoria Álvarez the ticket-clerk kept telling Elena how she was sure it was the same man whom she had seen bringing down a cripple into the Underground, and how she recalled the cripple's legs, which had dragged at an unnatural angle.

When Ángel Gallardo arrived to take over from Elena, she gave him an account of what had occurred. 'I'm going back to the Gobernación now,' she ended, 'to see if there's any news.'

'I expect it'll be a false trail,' he said cynically. 'If you're going by Metro, don't travel in the last coach. As it's the rush hour, those dirty old men, and young men, will pinch your bum in the crush when no one's looking.'

'I'll fend them off,' she said sternly. 'I've travelled on the Metro before, you know.'

SOL

As she emerged in the cool evening air at the Puerta del Sol, Elena was taken aback by a screaming newspaper fly-sheet: TERROR IN THE METRO! MANIAC AT LARGE! She bought a copy of the relevant paper and rushed up to Bernal's office, where Inspector Juan Lista stopped her in the outer office. 'The chief's gone to the lab to talk to Varga. I don't expect he'll be much longer.'

'Has Carlos Miranda rung in?'

'Yes, and the suspect gave him the slip at Atocha. I haven't been able to tell the *jefe* yet.'

When Bernal arrived, Elena held up the evening newspaper with the banner headlines surmounting a photograph of the second girl, who had been found murdered at Atocha Metro station.

'But they've published all this before, Elena!' exclaimed Bernal. 'Why are they raking it up again?'

'Read this bit, chief,' she said. '*Sources close to the DGS have revealed that there has been at least one other murder on the Metro which has not been made public by the authorities.*'

Bernal read this with mounting annoyance. 'Who has let this out? I'll get on to the Subsecretary at once.' He hurried into his office and dialled the number, tapping his notepad impatiently as he waited to be connected. 'Mr Secretary? This is Bernal. Have you seen the evening paper? You have? Could you possibly ring the editor and find out where he got the information about the first murdered girl? We haven't issued any statement about that case.' He listened for a while to the Subsecretary's reply. 'Yes, I realized at once it might cause a general panic, and I see the problem with the elections to be held in less than a fortnight. You'll let me know at once? I'm most grateful. Thank you, sir.'

Lista looked nervously at Elena. 'I'd better tell him about Miranda losing the suspect at Atocha.'

A few moments after Lista had gone into Bernal's inner office, the phone rang and Elena answered it. 'Yes, hold the line, Dr Peláez. The Superintendent is here.' She switched the phone through to Bernal.

'Peláez? ¿*Qué tal?*' He listened anxiously, then said, 'And did she get a good look at him? I see. Thick-set, thin-cheeked, dark receding hair. No hat. I see. And clean-shaven, you say? Is she sure of that? H'm. Yes. Well, thanks for letting me know so promptly. I'll be in touch.' He put down the receiver and turned to Lista, calling Elena to join them. 'Our man's more daring than we thought. The fellow that Miranda lost in El Brillante must have done a quick-change act, by taking off a false beard and moustache, and stowing his hat in his pocket or leaving it behind. Certainly he changed his appearance

sufficiently to fool Miranda. It appears that he has turned
up at the Instituto Anatómico Forense and has asked
Peláez's receptionist if he could see the corpse of the girl
brought in dead from the Metro, since he'd seen a photo
in the papers and wondered if it was a friend of his. The
receptionist knew, of course, that the corpse had been
identified as General Cabrera's daughter, but was
intelligent enough not to tell him so, and told him to wait
while she consulted Peláez. When they returned, he'd
done a bunk. From the description given, he seems to be
the same chap as Mari Luz Cabrera's girl-friend at the
Party headquarters had seen waiting for her on the last
night she had been seen alive.'

'You think he disguises himself when he comes through
Cuatro Caminos station to leave dolls or corpses on the
trains, then, *jefe*?' asked Elena. 'But why did he bother to
do so today?'

'Because he was on his way to the morgue to have a look
at his last victim,' suggested Bernal. 'But he realized he
was being followed, so he very boldly takes off his
disguise, in order to re-disguise himself, as far as his
shadower is concerned. It's a clever double-take.'

'What if there are two men involved, *jefe*?' asked Lista.

'It's hard to credit. Real psychopaths like this one
almost always work alone, and the chances of two of them
getting together to murder people are remote in the
extreme. In the text-books I can only recall those two
American cases in the 'thirties and four years ago, and
that couple in Northern England in the 'sixties.'

'But why would he want to see the girl's corpse again,
chief?' asked Elena.

'That's a very good question. What do you two think?'

'To gloat over it?' suggested Lista.

'Or to remove something incriminating from it?' Elena
put forward hesitantly.

'To gloat, perhaps,' said Bernal. 'But isn't it likely he

would have known that the body would be stripped and the autopsy performed?'

'But surely he'd have been shown the clothes and belongings, if he said he wasn't sure when he saw the face?' queried Elena.

'That's a possibility,' Bernal conceded. 'Ring Peláez and ask him to send over the things taken from Señorita Cabrera's body. Juan, perhaps you'd dig out the typed list of her personal possessions from the file? It should be with the forensic report.'

RETIRO

That night Bernal climbed up the steps at Retiro station with less sprightliness than usual, hardly seeing the other travellers who were hurrying home late from work. The turn the Metro murders was taking alarmed and exhilarated him at the same time. It was almost as though the killer wanted to be caught, or at least, to play a cat and mouse game with the police.

Clearly the psychopath wished to cause public panic, for a last-minute call he had received from the Sub-secretary had revealed that only one newspaper had been contacted about the first murder, and by an anonymous telephone call at that. When the sub-editor had checked with a friendly contact at the DGS, he had unwittingly agreed that there had been such a murder, not remembering that it was still the subject of a press ban. It seemed to Bernal very likely that the anonymous caller had been the murderer, but in that case why hadn't he also mentioned the two dolls, if he was the perpetrator of those as well? It was probable that he had also tipped the press off about the girl murdered at Atocha, María Luz Cabrera, though in that case it must imply that the killer had travelled on the same train as the corpse, perhaps moving to a different carriage before it was discovered; otherwise, how could he have known that the cadaver would have been spotted at Atocha, and not at an earlier or later station on Line 1?

Once more Bernal tried to form a mental picture of the psychopath from the few facts and hints available to him so far. A well-built man, about forty, with gaunt cheeks and receding hair, who had some knowledge of theatrical disguise and of wax-modelling, and who was confident enough to make a date with a girl and wait for her in the street. Then, because of some mental aberration, he murders her, in some convenient place—a workshop, garage or cellar—and then manifests a fixation about blood pouring from her mouth and about placing the corpse in a Metro train.

As he sipped his Larios *gin tonic* in Félix Pérez's bar, absently munching at a crab canapé from a plate on the counter, Bernal wondered what kind of ancient cerebral scar could lead to such a pattern of behaviour. What sort of peculiar sexuality could explain it? There was no sign that the murdered girls had been raped, or otherwise ill-treated, sexually or generally, apart from the murder method chosen, which seemed to have been particularly humane, within the gamut of *modi interficendi* Bernal had observed during his long career. Quite an unusual method, too; that, perhaps, was the best lead in this investigation. Bernal was especially seized with the urgency to apprehend the malefactor before another innocent girl lost her life.

He was not interested in personal glory, or the need to bolster his reputation, as younger or more ambitious men might be. After all, at 58 he could ask for a full pension at any time, and he had no desire to become a *superpolicía* as the newspapers were now dubbing one of the top superintendents. Under Franco, the names of the high-ranking policemen had rarely been published, which had given them an enormous cloak of anonymity, thereby frightening the populace. Furthermore, none of them could then ever have been brought to book for any abuse of power. Now, it was clear, with the incipient democracy, they were to take on a more public role, and some of his colleagues had already begun courting the agents of the media to ensure favourable treatment. This wasn't his style, Bernal considered. He had nothing serious to reproach himself for in his past actions, though he knew he had not always gone by the book, but rather by a hazy notion of justice, which he had never precisely analysed and which bore little relation to the strict legal definitions in the *Código Penal*.

Downing his gin, Bernal looked appreciatively at the old bar, with its little fretwork gallery painted a treacle brown, too small for anyone actually to stand on, its little row of pennants commemorating Real Madrid Football Club, and the tiny back room with two card-tables covered in green baize. He hoped they would never change it, but old Madrid was disappearing fast, and this was one of the few bars from the turn of the century still surviving in the Salamanca quarter. The proprietor was already putting up the shutters over the part of the bar counter that served customers directly on to the street as Bernal said good-night and walked out into the darkening chill.

As he let himself into the flat, the door struck some object inside that had not been there when he had left in the morning.

'Geñita? Where are you? I can't get in. There's something blocking the door.'

'Wait, Luis, don't push it open. You'll damage the piano.' His wife's voice came distantly from the terrace.

'We haven't got a piano,' he shouted.

She arrived breathless, clutching a plaster bust of

Beethoven, which she appeared to have been scrubbing with a brush. He observed that her face and arms were smudged with dust.

'What's been happening?' he asked, as she rearranged items of furniture sufficiently for him to enter. 'And where did all this come from?'

'From the lady on the floor below who died, you know, Doña Adoración. She and her late husband — may God rest their souls in His holy peace — were very musical, and her niece found her last wishes in a letter, in which she says she wanted us to have her upright piano and various other things.'

'But we can't play the piano, Geñita.'

'I know, but it's such lovely rosewood. Just look at it.' She ran her hand appreciatively over the very faded veneer. 'Over a hundred years old, and its got beautiful brass candelabra, which I'll want you to fix. I thought our grandchildren could play it when they come.'

'We've only got one grandson so far, Geñita,' he said quietly.

'But they'll have more for sure, and Diego will get married one of these days. There's just one problem: it won't turn the corner into the passageway. Do you think you could help me up-end it?'

'You realize it's got an iron frame, and weighs a ton. How did you get it this far?'

'The portress sent up her brother and his cousin who happened to drop in to see her, and they managed to get it up the stairs.'

'Where are you thinking of putting it?'

'I thought it would fit into the dining-room if we move the sideboard to the other wall.'

'Well, leave it for now. Diego will help me shift it in the morning. He's not in yet, I suppose?'

'He came in for lunch and took a two-hour siesta, then he said he had to go to the Calle de los Libreros to buy some books for his University course. He'll get a twenty per cent discount there.' This prospect afforded her considerable satisfaction. 'I gave him a five-hundred-peseta note. Was that too much?'

SOL

The next morning Bernal had a meeting with the Ministry Subsecretary and the Chief Commissioner of the Criminal Brigade. As usual, he felt uncomfortable in the elegant office overlooking the Puerta del Sol, and his eyes were drawn more to the ever-changing human mass on the pavements opposite than to the gilt-framed pier-glasses and the Isabelline desk, which bore little sign of any bureaucratic activity. The Subsecretary was new, having been transferred from Barcelona after his predecessor had fallen into political disgrace. The Commissioner, however, Bernal knew well, having worked in his team for a while in the early 'forties.

'What's worrying the Minister, Superintendent,' began the Subsecretary, waving them to rather unsafe-looking but elegant chairs, 'is that the travelling public will be panicked by the publicity over these murders in the Metro.'

'May I point out, Mr Secretary,' replied Bernal some-what sharply, 'that no murder has actually occurred in the Underground? First of all, two grotesque lifesize dolls were left in the trains: then two girls who had been murdered elsewhere were brought into the Metro, probably at Cuatro Caminos station. It's not as though women have actually been attacked on the trains.'

'I see that, Luis,' said the Commissioner, 'but the newspapers have not made that clear, and it's certain that they've succeeded in rousing public opinion.'

'You'll realize, Commissioner, that I haven't got anything like the manpower to patrol the stations and trains, even on Lines 1 and 2, where our man seems to be operating. Will the Minister authorize a full-scale operation?'

'I think he will, if we propose it. How many men would it take?' queried the Subsecretary.

'Well, if you're thinking of uniformed men travelling on the trains and patrolling the platforms in order to restore public confidence, it would take at least four hundred, counting one man on each train in motion and one on each platform at the seventy-eight stations. If you want them in pairs, it would be double that figure, of course. If they have to work two shifts, you can quadruple it. And what purpose would they serve, other than reassurance? They won't help to catch the murderer, who would naturally spot them at once. It may cause him to curtail his activities for the time being, and I see that that would be an advantage with the general elections in less than ten days. But have we enough men in Madrid to cover such an operation?'

'The Minister will authorize reinforcements from the provinces, Superintendent,' said the Subsecretary. 'But he has pointed out how difficult that would be with all the election meetings and possible political disorders.'

'What if we compromise on two uniformed men in every station on Lines 1 and 2, in two shifts, and one man at each of the others? There'd have to be more at the busy central interchanges, of course,' Bernal added. 'That might be sufficient to restore public confidence. I don't really see the point of the men travelling on the trains, since they'd not be likely to be in the right coach at the right moment, and the stations are pretty close together on the whole.' The Commissioner nodded his agreement. 'Also, I wouldn't want Cuatro Caminos station too heavily patrolled,' Bernal went on, 'or our surveillance there will be futile. We think we had a sighting of the suspect yesterday, and apparently he walked into the Forensic Institute as cool as you like, asking to see the corpse of his last known victim. Unfortunately he hopped it before the staff there could get on to us.'

'Do you think this is just one maniac operating alone, Bernal?' asked the Subsecretary.

'I've discussed the possible psychological motives with Dr Peláez, and he thinks it's a clear case of a homicidal psychopath, with some very strange quirks, such as the bag of blood placed in the mouths of the victims after death. Not to mention the obsession with the underground railway. It's extremely unlikely that he has an accomplice.'

'If you wish, Luis,' said the Commissioner, 'I'll see to the organization of the uniformed men's patrols in the way you've suggested. That will leave you free to concentrate on locating the suspect. What sort of description of him can we give to the men?'

'That's a very difficult problem. He has commonly disguised himself with a beard and moustache, but two female witnesses have seen him very briefly, apparently undisguised. The first is a party worker who was a friend of María Luz Cabrera, the General's daughter, and the other is Peláez's receptionist. I'll arrange for them to help to make a Photofit picture. But he may try some other way of disguising himself. More important is that they should investigate anyone aiding, or even carrying, a cripple. This will cause some mistaken challenges, of course, but it will be worth it if one of the uniformed men should catch him red-handed.'

On his return to his cramped and dusty office overlooking the busy side-street called the Calle de Carretas, Bernal decided to call a full conference of his team, including Dr Peláez, Varga the technician and Prieto of Fingerprints, at 1 p.m.

GARCÍA NOBLEJAS

The sun felt hot that morning, despite the breeze which blew along the Avenida de los Hermanos García Noblejas, the avenue with such a cumbersome name which led from the Cross of the Fallen at the end of the Calle de Alcalá to the suburb of San Blas. At its north-western end began the rich, upper-class, landscaped estates, but from Ciudad Lineal Metro station south-eastwards the wide avenue ran between hastily constructed working-class apartments, though from the occasional plantings of trees in the baked-mud spaces between the apartment-blocks, they clearly belonged to the upper end of that social group.

The small market behind the avenue really consisted of an L-shaped series of single-storey shops, and, apart from two bakeries, two *churrerías* which belched forth black smoke at breakfast-time when the coils of pancake-mixture were poured into boiling oil, and a draper's shop, most of them had been converted into bars. Telesforo the hunchbacked lottery-ticket seller did the rounds of these bars every lunch-time to catch the workers who had dropped in for a quick *caña* of beer; everyone knew him, and he was often treated to a drink, his favourite tipple being an alcoholic *bíter*—a concoction of wine with angostura served from a tiny bottle with a yellow label.

Telesforo, though he had no grasp of economic theory, had begun to notice how the growing unemployment and inflation actually increased his sales and therefore the proceeds from the ten per cent commission he added to the face value of the official tickets. The more hard up people were, the more they gambled. Most of these bars were inches deep in tote tickets, sold by the barman at five pesetas each, for a few prizes of between 125 and 1,000 pesetas. The locals called these tickets *cromos*, because they usually bore inside a blurred and badly coloured picture of a model in a saucy pose.

He was amazed how a gambling fever had struck the population in the working-class districts since Franco's death had loosened things up. The national lottery he sold was traditional, of course, since the eighteenth century (though he was not aware of that). But he viewed the recent incursions of *quinielas* or football pools, bar totes, tombolas, and now bingo halls as detrimental to his trade. Still, the seven bars in this small market had netted him 350 pesetas' commission and five free drinks in the space of half an hour.

He made his way across the street to García Noblejas Metro station, intending to go to the Barrio de la Concepción to have lunch with his sister. The steps leading down from the street were littered with election pamphlets, and in the booking-hall two women were handing out fly-sheets bearing a picture of Trotsky which were issued by one of the extreme left-wing parties officially forbidden to take part in the elections. Telesforo presented his yellow worker's return ticket for stamping by the *taquillera*, with whom he exchanged a cheery greeting, and started down the marble-lined staircase to the west-bound platform, direction *América*. All this line, Line 7, was new, and he thought it a shame the coloured wall-tiles were being encrusted with election stickers and sprayed-on slogans.

After a long wait, the sleek dark blue and light blue underground train entered the station almost silently, emitting only a hiss from its air brakes, and when the doors opened, Telesforo ensconced himself comfortably in one of the red padded seats in what appeared to be an empty carriage. He busied himself in counting his money and the remaining lottery tickets, and it was some time before he noticed the oddly dressed, tall girl slumped in a seat in the far corner.

The train emitted an efficient whistle, and accelerated

very quickly out of García Noblejas station. Engrossed in his calculations, Telesforo did not look up when the train stopped at Ascao, where no one got in. This was hardly surprising, since most people would be at work until 2 or 2.30 p.m. At the next station, Pueblo Nuevo, where there was an interchange with Line 5, the few remaining passengers in the other carriages got out to take a train to the city centre.

CONCEPCIÓN

Telesforo the hunchback gathered his tickets together as the train slowed to enter Concepción station, and he was surprised to find that the girl was no longer in sight, although she hadn't passed him on her way out. As he made his way towards the door, he looked over the seat and discovered her sprawled on the floor of the coach. His heart suddenly beat much faster as he saw the light-coloured blood trickle from her mouth, and his gorge rose at the much darker blood running down her nylon stockings from under her short, black leather skirt.

SOL

At one o'clock that day, all the members of Bernal's group, together with Varga and Prieto, were assembled in the large outer office. They were awaiting the arrival of Dr Peláez, in order to review the whole of the available evidence about the Metro murderer. Behind Bernal on the long wall hung a very large plan of the Metropolitan Railway, which had the seven lines marked in different colours, superimposed on a grid map of the city.

After a few minutes had passed, Peláez arrived breathless, mopping his bald head which was shining with perspiration.

'Sorry I'm late, Bernal. Had to sew up a cadaver and make it presentable for the relatives. I've brought the reports you wanted.'

'It's very good of you to spare the time, Peláez. These Metro murders are starting to cause a sensation and the Minister is concerned about a possible panic. He has authorized squads of uniformed men to patrol the platforms, though they will hardly help us catch the killer. I gather the suspect paid you a visit yesterday.'

'Apparently so, though I didn't catch sight of him myself. Why did he come to the lab, eh? To gloat over her?'

'It's been suggested he may have left something incriminating in the clothes, and therefore went along to try to extract it. Perhaps you'd give us your report on them, Varga, now you've had time to examine them closely.'

The stocky, black-haired technician opened his bundle of files and took out the top one. 'Well, chief, I've been over all the garments very carefully, not only those belonging to the two murdered girls, but also those found on the two dummies earlier. After your request yesterday, I examined all María Luz Cabrera's belongings with special care once more. I went over all the clothes with a vacuum cleaner, item by item, and now have the analyst's reports on the dust and débris. There are four main substances in common in all the items.' There was an expectant silence as Varga cleared his throat. 'Apart from ordinary household and street dust, there is a type of saprophytic mould common to all the garments, except for the Ledesma girl's red scarf. This fungal growth suggests that the clothes were kept in a damp, airless place.'

'Is there any way of telling for how long?' asked Bernal.

'For some weeks at least, or even a month or so,' replied Varga.

'Well,' said Bernal, 'that seems to confirm the theory that the clothes were bought in an old-clothes shop or in the Rastro flea-market. Clearly all of them came from the same place, and none of them belonged to the murdered girls, apart from the scarf, which Paloma Ledesma's mother identified as belonging to her daughter.'

'We should be a bit cautious, chief,' Varga went on, 'because this mould would form in most clothing stored anywhere damp, such as a cellar, if there was the right level of temperature.'

'But it takes a few weeks to form, from what you say,' replied Bernal, 'and there clearly wasn't time for that to occur between each girl's disappearance and the discovery of her body.'

'No, chief, but the clothes could have been possessed by the murderer for a long time and stored in a damp place.'

'That's true,' Bernal admitted, 'but if we have no stronger lead, we should question all the old-clothes dealers.'

Miranda, Lista and Ángel Gallardo winced at one another discreetly, while Elena feigned not to notice their wry faces.

'There's something else, jefe,' said Varga. 'All the outer clothing contained cement dust, and also some traces of a thermoplastic material, probably polystyrene in its glass-like form. The fragments appear to be in the form of a sawdust, suggesting that they are the residue of the plastic sheets cut or sawn to make the dummies.'

They all pondered on this statement, then Bernal ventured, 'All this seems to imply that the killer lured the two girls to the place where he constructed the dummies, and after killing them, stripped the bodies and put old clothes on them. But you said there were four substances found on all the clothes, Varga.'

'Yes, chief, and the fourth one is the most puzzling. There is a vegetal matter, which appears to be pollen from a plant we haven't yet been able to identify, but we've sent a sample to the Botanical Institute to see if they can help. This substance was also on Paloma Ledesma's scarf, unlike the other three substances.'

'Well, well, curiouser and curiouser,' commented Bernal, gazing round at the younger detectives who looked at one another doubtfully. 'Can anyone suggest an explanation?'

Lista, who often showed intuitive or rather deductive skill, was the first to speak. 'Perhaps the murderer has a hall or sitting-room where these flowers are to be found, and there the girls are brought first of all. Then they are murdered and taken to a garage or workshop which has a concrete floor, where the killer made the dummies. Later they are brought back through the place where the flowers are when they are dressed in the old clothes.'

This explanation seemed to meet with general approval.

'Do we know exactly how he kills his victims, chief?' asked Miranda.

Bernal looked at Peláez, who now opened his files of reports. 'He smothers them, but in the second case the Cabrera girl was given a fatal injection of cocaine. What worries me is the third person who has probably been murdered.'

'A third person?' echoed Elena wonderingly.

'Well, I don't think he could have extracted so much blood of B negative type, to fill the four sacs which he put into the mouths of the dummies and the cadavers, from a living person without fatal effects. What have the hæmatologists told you, Varga?' asked Peláez.

'You're right, sir, unless the blood was extracted over a long period of time. It's a very rare group, which doesn't correspond to that of either of the victims we have found so far. The tests have been complicated by the fact that the killer mixed the blood for the plastic bags with trichloroethylene, which he used as a solvent to stop it clotting. That makes it more difficult to tell its age. They've tried the new Gm. tests used for dried blood-stains, as well as all the latest tests for haptoglobins, enzyme systems and protein groups. The analysts are sure it derives from a white European, in early adulthood. They can't say more than that, but they have a "blood-print" which they can try to match with other samples from the same body, or the body itself, of course, if you find it.'

'This garage, or workshop, which he has,' mused Bernal, 'must be a grotesque place. He makes dummies there, he takes corpses into it, perhaps keeping one there; it must give out strange smells and noises from his activities.' Elena shuddered visibly, remembering how close she had been to the suspect. 'Can no one have noticed, no relative or neighbour?' asked Bernal. 'What sort of premises can they be?'

Navarro spoke for the first time in the discussion. 'A house with a basement where he lives alone? But that would be hard to find near Cuatro Caminos.'

'Exactly,' said Bernal. 'There are mostly apartment blocks, or at least, houses divided into flats with porters in the downstairs hallways. They're generally so nosy that they'd spot anything odd, such as a bad smell, or dummies and bodies being carried in and out. Of course, some houses now have automatic porters, which doesn't help us. As you can see from the map,' he said, taking up a wooden pointer and indicating the Metro stations where the dummies and bodies had been found, which were marked with tiny coloured flags, 'Cuatro Caminos station must have been the point of ingress. The suspect has been spotted there twice. But how did he get the dummies and bodies as far as the station entrance?'

'By car or van,' suggested Miranda.

'But it's not easy to park near the station steps,' objected Ángel, 'at least not for long, without getting a parking ticket or having the vehicle towed away by the Municipal Police crane.'

'And he seems to have accompanied the dummies and bodies for part or all the journey,' added Bernal.

'He must be very strong to have carried the girls' bodies down those stairways,' said Elena. 'If he's the man I saw, it's possible—he was tall and broad-shouldered, and remarkably lithe and sure-footed. But he would surely have had to rest the corpse every so often, and it's strange no one noticed.'

'Especially when you consider the time of day he dumped the Cabrera girl,' Bernal pointed out, 'in the middle of the morning rush-hour.'

'Is there no other way he could have got them down?' asked Lista. 'There are coach-sheds at Cuatro Caminos, aren't there? Is there no private entrance for the employees which he might have used at a particular time without being spotted?'

'That's an excellent point,' commented Bernal. 'We must ask the Metro Director at once and investigate the station thoroughly for clues.' He looked round at his small team with a wry look. 'We've got very little to go on, as you'll have realized. I now suggest two other lines of inquiry, both of which will be troublesome for you.' He turned to Miranda. 'I would like you, Carlos, to take Elena on a tour of the old-clothes dealers, to see if they can recognize any of the garments found on the dummies or the murder victims, or remember the man who may have bought them. He may have picked them up all together as a job lot.' Turning to Gallardo, he said, 'Ángel, I want you to remain in charge of the surveillance at Cuatro Caminos for the moment, though with the *grises* patrolling the platforms from this afternoon, I don't expect our suspect to show his nose for the time being. Juan,' he went on, addressing Lista, 'I want you to organize a house-to-house enquiry around Cuatro Caminos station. You can ask for six more plainclothesmen from the central pool. You'd best question the porters and local shopkeepers about a garage or workshop which someone might be using for modelling construction or sculpture, since we know he uses sheets of polystyrene in opaque glass-like form. If only we knew what sort of flowers the pollen came from, they could be searched for, but keep your eyes open for anything that might fit. And, of course, ask about the suspect in both of his manifestations: we should shortly have the Photofit pictures of him with and without his beard and moustache. I don't suppose you've found any more fingerprints, Prieto?'

The others cocked their ears on hearing this question.

'No, chief, nothing apart from the small partial print on the Ledesma girl's scarf, which is so fragmentary it can only be used in poroscopy, should you find more prints, or the man himself. He must wear gloves most of the time when he's handling incriminatory matter.'

'Well, thank you. Can any of you think of anything I've missed?'

No one volunteered any further suggestion. 'Paco, you can man the office, and I'll talk to the Metro Director before going to Cuatro Caminos coach-sheds to talk to the employees. The surveillance team is still there, isn't it?'

'Yes, *jefe*,' said Ángel, 'I told them to wait for further instructions.'

CONCEPCIÓN

The station-master gazed in horror at the bloodstained corpse of the tall, titian-haired girl, which was lying in the third carriage of the brand-new train standing at his west-bound platform. He had put the lottery-ticket seller to sit in his office while he telephoned the Control at Avenida de América to suspend the service and arrange for the train to be sealed and taken to the coach-sheds there. The driver and guard had joined him at the doorway of the carriage.

'The maniac's got another victim, then, by the looks of it,' commented the driver, a morose man who looked as though he had the peptic ulcer that was an occupational hazard. 'Did you see this girl get on the train?' he asked the guard, who was a much younger man, addicted to adult comics which he pored over between stations, and one of which was now folded under his left arm.

'No, but remember I was three coaches away. I didn't see anything out of the ordinary on any of the station TV screens either.' On all the platforms on this, the Company's latest and most up-to-date line, closed-circuit television cameras and screens enabled the guard, who travelled in the front coach immediately behind the driver's cab, to see the whole of the platform without getting out or craning his neck when sounding the whistle and closing the doors at each station.

'She was very tall, wasn't she?' remarked the driver.

'Not a bad looker,' said the station-master. 'Nice legs she had. Why would anyone want to knock her off?'

'She looks to me as though she was a bit of a *puta*,' said the driver. 'Look at her painted fingernails and toenails. A decent girl doesn't go out like that. And her hair's dyed.'

'Go on, you're behind the times,' jeered the guard. 'All of 'em go about like that now. If this maniac only wants to bump off whores, he'll have a hard job to sort 'em out from the virgins, what's left of 'em.'

The phone rang in the station-master's office, and he hurried back to answer it. He then returned with orders from Central Control for the train to be taken direct to the coach-sheds, where the Metro Security men would arrive shortly.

CUATRO CAMINOS

Bernal got off the old red-and-cream Metro train at Cuatro Caminos with Ángel, and went up the stairs with him to give instructions to the plainclothesmen who were carrying on the surveillance at the entrance. He had learned from the Director of the Metropolitan Company that there was a workmen's entrance to the coach-sheds in the Calle de Fernández Villaverde, and it was this he now wished to inspect. Although the murderer appeared to have carried at least one of the dummies through the ticket-hall and down the passenger staircase before leaving it on a train, Bernal wanted to see if it was feasible for him to have taken the corpses of the girls by an easier route and put them into the trains before they went into service.

As they emerged on to the Calle de Bravo Murillo, he turned to Ángel and said, 'I see what you mean about the parking here. It wouldn't have been possible for the killer to have left a vehicle on such a busy street as this while depositing the corpses in the trains. But let's have a look around the corner, near the coach-shed entrance.'

There, they saw, was a perfect spot for parking a vehicle, in front of an apartment block.

'We'd better check the security at the Metro employees' entrance,' said Ángel.

They found they could enter with ease, for there was no doorman, and from the gloomy cavern below came the clanging of repair work and the hiss of water-hoses from the automatic train-wash machine.

'I'd put my money on this route, *jefe*,' said Ángel. 'Look, there's even a lift which they probably use to take down spare parts and pieces of machinery.'

'Let's go down in it and see if we are challenged, then,' suggested Bernal.

In fact they had emerged from the lift at the lower level and had gone a considerable distance between the parked carriages before anyone came up to them.

'I'm the foreman,' said a harassed-looking man with grease-marks on his face, hands and blue overalls. 'Can I be of any assistance to you gentlemen?'

Bernal produced his DGS badge, and the foreman said he was expecting him, since the Director's office had phoned.

'Could you just show us around?' Bernal asked him. 'Perhaps you could explain in what order the coaches are brought in and what happens to them.'

'Well, if they need repair, they are shunted to the workshop over there.' He indicated the far corner of the enormous underground hall. 'When they need washing or disinfecting, they go to one of the central bays. The ones parked nearest here are complete trains which are used in the morning and evening rush hours, when the frequency of the service is increased. Two shifts of women clean and brush out the interiors at night and in the early morning before the trains go into service. The drivers and guards pick them up at the control exit.'

'And do these trains only go out on to Line 2, which runs from here to Ventas, or are they used also on Line 1, which only passes through this station?' inquired Bernal.

'Mainly on Line 2, but in busy periods they may be required for Line 1 and the train started from this station. But normally Line 1 trains start from the Plaza de Castilla, or from Portazgo at the southern end of that line.'

'Now, it's been explained to me,' said Bernal, 'that

each train that passes on each line is given a number in a series so that the station-masters can report to Central Control at Sol the position of each one. Can you tell me what happens to the extra trains inserted into Line 1 from these coach-sheds? Are they given a special number?'

'Yes, sir. The traffic manager here rings Central Control to find out the right moment to put in the extra train, and they tell him the number to put, "17*bis*" or "18*bis*" for example. He then gives the driver a cardboard plaque to display in the front window, which informs the station-masters of the train's order along the line.'

'And do you keep a record of the permanent number of each of the six coaches that makes up a train, and is that logged against the temporary order-number that the train receives when it enters service?'

'I keep the series numbers of the coaches on each train from this depot, and give them in summary form to the Traffic Manager, M19/R313 for example, the first and last coaches of a particular train. His log-book contains a record of the time of departure and the convoy-number allotted to the train.'

'That's excellent,' said Bernal. 'We shall be wanting to consult the log for particular trains on particular dates. How many people work here on an average day?'

'More than forty of us in two shifts most of the day. More when the cleaners are in.'

'Is there a doorkeeper or someone who checks the workers in and out?' asked Ángel.

'Not since we've had an automatic time-clock. We just punch these cards in it as we enter and leave these days.' He showed them a long buff card which he pulled out from the pocket of his overalls.

Bernal asked him, 'Do you think it possible for someone to bring a large package down here and put it in a train without being spotted?'

'You mean a body? Yes, I've read the newspapers,' he

said with a nervous grin. 'I've thought about it and it could happen, especially after the cleaners have gone and the train doors are left open before departure. What with the noise and the bad lighting, we probably wouldn't notice someone slipping in, and there are so many places to hide among the piles of spares and in the archways round the walls.'

'Well, that's an honest answer. Thank you. I'm going to send three plainclothesmen down here, one on each shift, to keep a discreet watch, just in case the suspect tries to use this route again. You've been most helpful.'

As they returned to the street, Bernal confessed to Ángel, 'I've slipped up badly in this enquiry. I was put off normal procedure by the sighting of the suspect with the dummy by that woman ticket-clerk. What we must do is to check the provenance of each train in which a body or a dummy was found. Will you ring Navarro and get him to read you the coach number in each incident from the reports we have, and the approximate times. The foreman and Traffic Manager here will then look up their logs and tell you where those trains originated, that is, either from the Plaza de Castilla on Line 1 or from here on Lines 1 or 2. Can you think of anything else we ought to do?'

'There is the vehicle he may have used,' said Ángel. 'Surely he didn't carry the bodies along the street.'

'Quite right,' said Bernal. 'We want more men to note down the numbers of all parked vehicles in this immediate neighbourhood, and then check on the owners.'

'And the traffic wardens, *jefe*? Shall I get on to the Municipal Police Traffic Section and ask for all the parking tickets issued in this vicinity?'

'Yes, but start by asking only for those issued on the days when the dummies and bodies were found. That should reduce the list. You'll be able to eliminate most

of the overnight car-parkers who live in the neighbourhood—though, of course, the murderer could be one
of them. I'm more interested in strange cars parked here
on each of those occasions. I'll see you in the office after
lunch. *Hasta luego.*'

As Ángel went off into the underground-station
entrance, Bernal looked up Bravo Murillo for a taxi, with
a strong feeling of locking the stable-door after the horse's
departure.

TRIBUNAL

As he settled back into the taxi, Bernal realized he could
have got to Tribunal more quickly on the Metro, but on
due consideration he felt he'd had enough of its peculiar,
warm, metallic odour and unhealthy air for one day. It
was still only two o'clock, so he would have time for *tapas*
at the Cafetería Pablos, where he asked the driver to put
him down. The weather was much hotter now, having
performed one of those quick changes for which Madrid
was famous, whereby a rise of 15° or 20° Centigrade was
possible from the early hours of the morning to early
afternoon.

He sipped a gin and tonic and picked at a small saucer
of mussels in brine, while gazing through the large
smoked-glass windows at the children playing in the
Gardens of the Architect Ribera opposite. The Calle de
Barceló was one of the pleasantest spots near the city
centre, he reflected, if only the Ayuntamiento didn't keep
sending labourers to dig it up.

He went to the telephone at the back of the café and
rang Eugenia to tell her he wouldn't be home for lunch.
He then ordered *Plato Combinado No. 5* from the menu,
which turned out to consist of a veal steak, two fried eggs,

three ham croquettes and a tomato and lettuce salad. After a coffee and brandy, he paid the bill and went down the street to the apartment block where his secret, second flat was located. There he found Consuelo making herself some soup from a packet, which she left to give him a hug.

'I've read about the Metro murders, Luchi,' she said. 'I've decided not to travel on the Underground for the time being.'

'That's the sort of alarm the murderer appears to want to create, love,' said Bernal wearily. 'He hasn't actually killed anybody on a train, as far as we know. He only dumps the corpses there.'

'And how many have there been?' she asked. 'The papers hint darkly at more than you've been letting on.'

'Two bodies and two dummies, so far.'

'Dummies?'

'Yes, lifesize dolls made to look like real victims. We also have good reason to suppose that there's a third victim, whose cadaver we haven't found yet. Are you sure you want to hear all about this with your soup?'

'I suppose you think it would be more appropriate to tell me about it in bed afterwards,' she retorted. 'I'd rather have the gory details with the soup.'

After listening to all the facts as they were known to the police and the inquiries that were afoot, she thought for a time without saying anything, then she asked him, 'Have you wondered how he's managing to lure the girls to wherever it is that he kills them?'

'Only that it must seem quite normal to them. After all, he was waiting for Mari Luz Cabrera as though they had a date.'

'What about the drugs angle? Could he be a pusher?'

'I've had Superintendent Tomás go through the Narcotics files: the girls didn't have a record, and he says there's no obvious connection. But I'll ask Elena and

Carlos Miranda to look at the mug-shots he's got, although they only saw him disguised. Peláez's receptionist could also have a try; she saw him without the beard.'

'Trust that Elena to lose the suspect,' crowed Consuelo, who had resented the competition she imagined the new female inspector represented. 'She's just a greenhorn.'

'It's not fair to blame her,' replied Bernal patiently, 'she only fingered him for Miranda, who's the best shadower we've got.'

'If it's not drugs, could it be an abortion racket?' Consuelo mused.

'According to Peláez there were no recent signs of illegal operations, and neither girl was pregnant. In any case, the Cabrera family is so rich they would have paid for their daughter to go abroad and have it done legally.'

'Then politics? Both girls were working for left-wing parties. Perhaps he's a right-wing fanatic and just chooses them arbitrarily from any pro-marxist organization.' She shivered. 'You'd better come with me to the socialist rally next Monday at the Rayo Vallecano team's stadium at El Portazgo. I want to hear Felipe González's eve of poll speech, and you'll have to come to protect me.'

'I wish you wouldn't go to those political meetings, Consuelo. The whole country's gone mad, as though the revolution's round the corner, and you must see that it won't last five minutes once the post-election disillusion happens. It was just like this in 1931.'

'And I bet you were waving red banners with the best of them then, Luchi.' He thought she had an over-romantic view of his youth. 'Come on, own up to your Trotskyist past.'

'I can't, because I was only twelve at the time. But yes,' he conceded, 'I admit we felt a bit like the kids today, hoping to turn things upside down overnight. But you're too experienced to get swept overboard by all this.'

'I suppose I ought to be, but I can't help getting caught up in it, of having that feeling of history being made and not wanting to miss out on it. Come on, take me to the Vallecas rally next Monday. No one will spot us in such a crush.'

'All right,' Luis relented, 'if I'm free, I will. Now, what about a quick siesta before I go out sleuthing again?'

'Come off it! The Academy will have to redefine *siesta* in its dictionary when its members get to know what you've got in mind!'

SOL

Inspector Paco Navarro took the call from Metro Security at 2.10 p.m., and was driven to near-panic. He ordered the security men not to move or touch the girl's body in the train, which had been taken to Avenida de América station. Then he tried to locate Superintendent Bernal by telephone. His wife Eugenia informed him, rather drily, Paco thought, that Luis had just rung her to say he wouldn't be in for lunch, she didn't know where from. When he had rung Cuatro Caminos station, Ángel had told him the chief had left in a taxi at 1.45. Navarro had noticed on other occasions that Bernal could be hard to find in the early afternoons and had wondered about it. No doubt he was comfortably ensconced in a bar somewhere, sipping *cañas* with his old friends.

In desperation, Paco called the Instituto Anatómico Forense, and asked for Dr Peláez. But he too had slipped out for lunch.

'Has he gone home?' he asked the receptionist, who, he remembered, was a dark-haired beauty from Seville. She had tried hard to conquer her Andalusian accent, but sufficient of it broke through to give what she said a slightly comical tone.

'I shouldn't think so, Inspector,' she replied, 'he usually slips out to the Mesón at the corner of Drumen and Atocha. But he should be back by three, as he has an autopsy to do.'

Navarro explained that he hadn't yet located Superintendent Bernal, but he told her about the corpse at Avenida de América station.

'I'll tell the doctor as soon as he arrives. Presumably he'll meet the Superintendent at the scene of the incident.'

Navarro wondered whether all corpses, however gruesome, were just 'incidents' to her, seeing them wheeled in and out each and every day, as she did.

He tapped his pencil anxiously on his notepad, then decided to leave messages for Varga the technician and Prieto of Fingerprints, though it didn't seem likely there would be a lot of fingerprinting to do at the scene. He vacillated over whether to inform the judge of instruction who was on duty today; he would be from the Juzgado No. 17. He sighed, and rang down to the uniformed man on the door to send out for a *bocadillo* of mountain ham and Manchegan cheese and a bottle of Mahou five-star beer. It was going to be a long afternoon.

AVENIDA DE AMÉRICA

At 3.50 p.m. in the coach-sheds at Avenida de América station, the police photographer was at work, while Inspector Quintana from Chamartín district *comisaría* stood near by, accompanied by two grey-uniformed policemen.

Varga arrived and showed his credentials to Quintana, whom he did not know.

'Superintendent Bernal will be here shortly, Inspector.

I won't disturb the body until he and Dr Peláez arrive, but I can start examining the interior of the coach when the photographer has finished.'

'Very good,' said Quintana. 'I rang the DGS at once when this was reported to our station in the Calle de Cartagena. Metro Security naturally alerted the nearest district police station, as well as the Superintendent's office. It seems clear that this is one of the maniacal killings Bernal is already investigating. I haven't permitted anyone to enter since I arrived, except the photographer.'

'Who found her?' asked Varga.

'A lottery-ticket seller, whom I'm holding for Superintendent Bernal to question. He's already made a deposition.'

Varga began to rig up additional lighting for the forensic search, as the photographer finished taking his shots by flash.

'I'll stand by until the doctor comes,' he told Varga, 'since he'll want more shots when he's turned her over.'

'I don't think the position of the body is going to be very important,' said Inspector Quintana, 'because the witness says that she fell off the seat where she had been in a sitting position only when the train arrived at Concepción station, and that was over two hours ago.'

'Well, if the blood is still liquid, the post-mortem hypostasis could well have altered during that time,' commented Varga. 'Dr Peláez won't be very pleased.'

That gentleman now arrived, bearing his large black gladstone bag, and waved a cheery greeting.

'Bernal not here yet?' he said, looking around. 'I told him there'd be more victims if he didn't get the psychopath quickly.' His protuberant eyes gleamed exaggeratedly behind his thick pebble lenses as he looked in at the girl's corpse. 'Fell off the seat, did she? How long ago, Quintana?'

'At about 1.35 p.m., at Concepción station. The train was then brought here. We haven't touched her, but she's been photographed *in situ* and Varga's just beginning the forensic search.'

'Don't suppose you'll find much, Varga,' said Peláez. 'Not when so many people troop in and out of these trains all day.' He bent over the corpse. 'Tall, big-boned girl, wasn't she?' He grasped the left wrist of the cadaver. 'Quite a bit of cooling has occurred.' After lifting each eyelid in turn, he said, 'Pupils already in post-mortem relaxation.'

Inspector Quintana, watching from the doorway, suddenly realized that Peláez wasn't speaking for his or Varga's benefit, but into a tiny microphone hanging on a cord around his neck, which had a wire leading to the doctor's coat pocket. Good idea, he thought, saves him bringing a secretary around.

Peláez turned the corpse half over. 'Usual lot of blood from the mouth, which we've seen in the other two cases.' He called the photographer over. 'Take some shots now, will you?' Then, with a pair of tweezers, he removed from between the victim's teeth a transparent plastic sac which oozed blood. Afterwards he raised the skirt and looked for the source of the bloodstains on the legs. 'H'm, some wound in the private parts; not a lot of blood, though. Taken to raping them now, has he?' He turned the cadaver over and inserted a thermometer into the rectum, and hung another on the back of a seat to check the air temperature inside the carriage.

While he waited, Peláez went to the doorway to chat to Varga, who was on his hands and knees going over the floor with a magnifying glass. 'Where's Bernal, then?'

'Navarro says he couldn't contact him an hour ago. Perhaps he's having lunch with someone. He usually phones in at four.'

Glancing at his watch, Peláez went back to the corpse

and started taking samples of the bloodstains from the mouth and from the legs, and labelling the small tubes. He also inscribed a large white label which he tied to the girl's right foot. 'No sign of a purse or handbag, Varga. And there are no pockets in the jacket or blouse. I think we'll have a problem doing an ID.'

'She's dressed differently from the others,' observed Varga. 'Apart from the jacket, which is pretty tatty, the blouse and leather skirt don't look as if they've come from an old clothes dealer. And this time there's no raincoat or hat.'

'That's because of the weather,' said Peláez. 'It would have attracted too much attention on a warm day if he'd muffled her up. Heavily painted, wasn't she?' He looked at the face with the now collapsed nostrils. 'And the fingernails and toenails. Good-time girl, do you think?'

'Could be,' said Varga. 'The hairs's clearly dyed that titian shade. She must have been quite stunning with those bold facial features.'

Peláez was now noting down the body temperature and checking it against the air temperature in the coach. 'H'm, almost five degrees down, and it's fairly warm in here — 21 degrees. So long as it's not a strangulation, or a rare case of fever or poisoning, in which the temperature rises for a time after death, we might guess that she's been dead for six to eight hours.' He felt the muscles of the neck and shoulders, and ran his fingers down the arms. 'Rigor has begun, but has not reached the forearms yet.' He turned to Inspector Quintana. 'In fairly warm conditions where the cadaver is dressed, it may not begin for up to six hours, and then takes about ten to twelve hours to become total.' He lifted the sleeves of the jacket and examined the inner part of the arms. 'One small injection-mark inside the left arm. Looks recent.' He lifted the skirt again and looked at the thighs. 'No, no marks there. Not an addict, then, or at least, not by injection.' He examined the dark staining in the lower part of the legs. 'Post-mortem hypostasis. Was in a sitting position for some time after death. I can't do much more here, Varga. Sooner I can cut her up in the lab the better. We'll have her lifted as soon as the duty judge gets here. Still no Bernal, eh?'

Shortly afterwards, the judge of instruction from the Juzgado de Guardia arrived, and conferred with Inspector Quintana. There was an awkward pause while they awaited the Superintendent, and the inspector offered round a packet of Rex cigarettes. The foreman of the coach-sheds approached them.

'I've just had a call, señores. The Director of the Metro and Superintendent Bernal are on their way down.'

Varga continued to collect dust samples and other débris from around the corpse. The employees gazed inquisitively at the official group from a discreet distance, while pretending to get on with their tasks. A sudden renewed hum of activity from them signalled the arrival of the Metro chief. Bernal came up to Quintana and shook hands.

'Sorry to be so late. Lunch-time is always the worst time to find people. Have you examined the corpse?'

'Only from a distance. I've let Varga and Dr Peláez do the detailed job. I didn't want to trample over the evidence and spoil things. It's clearly one of the Metro murders.'

Bernal respected Quintana, whom he had known for many years. One of the newer breed of DGS men from the 'fifties, he had a good record in detection since he'd been assigned to the Chamartín district. 'Thank you, Quintana, I appreciate your handing it straight over to us.'

The director blanched when he saw the girl's corpse through the carriage doorway. 'Can we keep this from the press, Superintendent? We've suffered enough publicity already, and now with the policemen on all the platforms . . .'

Bernal gently cut him short. 'We can't control it, because the murderer seems to be tipping off the newspapers himself. I'm surprised they aren't here already.' He went into the carriage with the judge of instruction and they conferred with Peláez.

'Is it clear that she was murdered elsewhere and brought into the carriage, doctor?' asked the judge.

'Almost certainly, because the plastic bag of blood was placed in the mouth when she was dead, or already unconscious, and that would have been difficult to do in public. To judge from the staining, she's been moved about considerably after death. Was in a sitting position for some time, to judge by the back of the thighs and the legs. And, of course, a witness saw the corpse fall from the seat to the floor—or at least, saw afterwards that it had fallen—as the train entered Concepción station at 1.35. I'd like to do the autopsy at once.'

'Of course, I'll authorize it now. You'll let me have a preliminary report, Bernal? Then we can transfer the matter to the Juzgado which handled the first Metro victim. Once you are sure that this person is a victim of the same series of crimes, of course.'

After the judge's departure, Bernal talked to the Metro director. 'I shall need to question the driver and guard of this train, and all the station-masters and ticket-clerks along the line. I'll also need to see the train's schedule of journeys. It looks as though it's going to be very difficult to pinpoint the station of ingress.'

'Do you think it possible the murderer could have brought the corpse down the stairs at one of the stations without the staff or the travelling public noticing?'

'It seems unlikely, on the face of it. In the other two cases, we now think the killer dumped the bodies at Cuatro Caminos coach-sheds. But this line does not link with Lines 1 and 2 at any point. It's a completely separate operation, isn't it?'

'Yes, and our latest and best line. Entirely automated system.'

'Then it's possible he brought this girl's body down at these coach-sheds, or at Las Musas, at the other end of the line. That's why we must find out how long this train has been in service today.'

'We'll find out at once,' said the director. 'I'll call the traffic manager over.'

Before being driven out to the Avenida de América, Bernal had had time to consult the large plan of the Metro system in his office when Navarro had given him the bad news. They had both been appalled to see that this new crime was discovered on a totally different line, and Bernal felt as though the murderer was constantly one step ahead of them. No sooner did they work out how he had introduced the bodies on to Lines 1 and 2 and put on a special surveillance at Cuatro Caminos, than the psychopath switched to Line 7.

The traffic manager arrived with the schedule book. 'This train, sir, number twenty-three it was in today's journey sequence, was used in the morning from the commencement of service until 11.30. Then it was withdrawn to this coach-shed and did not re-enter the system until 1.05, when a different crew took it out. A fault had developed in the brake warning-lights, but it was only a question of replacing a light-bulb, so I put it back into service when that had been done.'

'What is the journey time from here to Las Musas?' asked Bernal.

'Officially 16 minutes, 10 seconds, but it's sometimes longer if there's a delay in the signalling.'

'Let's get this straight,' said Bernal. 'If it left here at 1.05 on its second turn of duty, how long was it at Las Musas before setting out on the return journey?'

'Probably only two or three minutes. I'll check with the traffic controller there.'

'Then when the corpse was discovered at 1.35 at Concepción, that was the train's first return journey during its second tour of duty?'

'Oh yes, I thought you'd realized that, sir. Concepción is about two-thirds of the trajectory from Las Musas to América, so that if train twenty-three departed Las Musas at 1.23 or thereabouts, eleven or twelve minutes later it would have reached Concepción.'

'Well, that's very helpful. Can you show me where it was parked here during the late morning? Would the doors have been left open?'

'Just over there, in that parking bay. Yes, the electrician would have opened the doors when he was working on it. I'll get him over afterwards, if you like, Superintendent.'

'I'll ring through for one of my group to come and help me take statements. I'll want to talk to all those on duty here this morning, up to the time of the train's departure at five past one.'

Bernal telephoned Navarro from the traffic manager's office and asked him to send Ángel from Cuatro Caminos, or whomsoever he had available. The Metro director offered to arrange for a room to be placed at the murder team's disposal, and took his leave once the cadaver had been removed. Varga completed his search of the seat in front of which the body had lain.

Peláez, on his way out, took Bernal aside. 'There's no sign of drug addiction, but there's one injection-mark in the left arm. I'll send the urine, intestinal and gastric contents, some of the blood and five hundred grams of the brain and liver to the Institute of Toxicology for them to check for drugs or toxic substances. There's no external sign of violence, except for what appears to be a knife-wound in the vulva. I thought it was rape at first.'

'Would that wound have been enough to cause death?' asked Bernal. 'If so, he's changed his habits.'

'Yes, but I don't think it was. There was very little bleeding for such a wound. I think it was inflicted after death.'

'And the time of death?' Bernal asked the time-honoured question.

'I'll have to see the stomach contents first, though people breakfast at such disparate hours that it's not as helpful as lunch. Between 8 and 11 this morning? Will that help? It's just an estimate from the body temperature and the amount of rigor, but both methods are unreliable in themselves, as you know. Put together with the state of the stomach contents, they are somewhat more useful. I'll ring you later this evening from the Institute. *Hasta luego*,' and he rushed off.

After inspecting the security arrangements, or rather the lack of them, at the entrance to the coach-sheds, Bernal decided to return to his office and call off the door-to-door enquiry at Cuatro Caminos in order to recover part of his group to question the Metro employees at Avenida de América station.

SOL

That evening Navarro and Bernal gazed at the large map of the city in something approaching desperation.

'With that great distance between Cuatro Caminos and América, chief,' said Navarro, 'it would take many teams of men to do a house-to-house investigation. The area takes in a large stretch of the Castellana, as well as the Calles de Ríos Rosas, Joaquín Costa and parts of Serrano and Velázquez. It would be an enormous task.'

'We'll call off the enquiry around Cuatro Caminos

now, Paco. It's clear the killer has a vehicle and sees no problem in driving the corpses in broad daylight to any Metro coach-sheds he fancies. What I do want is an immediate surveillance on all the terminus points, especially the coach-shed entrances. We've been wasting our time at Cuatro Caminos ticket-hall, apparently, yet it was there that the *taquillera* pointed him out to Elena as the man she thought she had seen bringing in one of the dummies. Has anything come in about the old-clothes dealers?'

'Elena rang in to say there was no luck so far, *jefe*. She says she'll have to wait until the day after tomorrow to interview some of them, because they only turn up on Sunday mornings in the Rastro, and God only knows where they hang out in between. The Subsecretary has just telephoned, after seeing the incidents report with the news of the third corpse.'

'But the press reporters haven't rung?'

'No, chief, they don't appear to have got on to it yet.'

Navarro was wrong, however, because a special edition of the most sensational of the evening papers was even then rolling off the presses, and would be at the central news-stands by 7.15.

ATOCHA

In the chilly, white-tiled dissection room in the Calle de Santa Isabel, Dr Peláez was conducting the autopsy on the unknown girl found at Concepción station. As he worked, he dictated his report to his good-looking secretary who sat, with two cardigans round her shoulders, on a high stool near the door. He had already removed the organs which would be required by the toxicologist, and was now examining the genital wound under a glass. He asked the aged mortuary attendant to bring him a smaller scalpel, and with a skill that came from very long experience, laid open the area of the womb.

Suddenly he stopped dictating in mid-sentence, uttered a swear word which greatly surprised his secretary, and called the attendant to come and pull off his rubber gloves.

'María, I've got to call Bernal urgently, before he leaves the office. You can take a break for coffee.'

SOL

By 8 p.m., Ángel had got back to the office in the DGS building, clutching a copy of the extra edition of the popular evening newspaper.

'I expect you've seen this, *jefe*.'

The enormous black headlines screamed: — THIRD GIRL MURDERED IN METRO! Bernal scanned the sparse accompanying text in mounting annoyance.

'Reliable sources, indeed! One of the Metro employees has rung them and got five thousand pesetas for the tip-off. They've got no details, not even a description of the girl. And they think she was found at Avenida de América; they don't know it was Concepción. That points to an employee, don't you think?'

'What if it was the killer who rang them?' Navarro suggested tentatively.

'Unless he was on the same train, how would he have known which terminus the corpse would be taken to after being discovered?' objected Bernal. 'I specially asked the Subsecretary to get the newspaper editors to have all anonymous calls tape-recorded. That way we might get a voice-print of the murderer. I'll ring through now to ask

them to check with the night-desk of this rag, though I
expect they'll have gone home by now.'

Later, after arranging for some of the team to man the
temporary murder unit at Avenida de América during
the early morning, to interview the Metro employees
there, Bernal and Ángel were getting ready to leave when
Peláez rang.

'Bernal? Is that you?' the pathologist spoke somewhat
breathlessly. 'I've made an extraordinary discovery about
the latest Metro victim.'

'Well, go on, Peláez.'

'You noticed that there was a wound in the genital
area, as though a sharp object had been forced into the
vulva, probably after death? Well, I've just been
dissecting that region for a closer look at the internal
marks, to try to identify the weapon used. I have to tell
you that we are not dealing with the corpse of a woman.'

'Not a woman?' exclaimed Bernal.

'Not a real woman. The vagina consists of a surgical
reconstruction. There's no womb, and there are no
ovaries. I've never come across such a job myself, but I've
seen photographs of such, operations in the journals.
Probably done in Morocco — that's the usual place they go
to have it done, I believe. Quite skilful, too. It fooled me
at first, I can tell you.'

'You mean she's really a castrated man?' asked Bernal
incredulously.

Paco and Ángel pricked up their ears.

'More than that. An operated trans-sexual. I didn't
notice any sign of silicon implants in the breasts, but I'll
go back and search for them. The secondary features may
have been altered by continuous hormone treatment. No
sign of a beard. The reconstructed external sexual
characteristics would have fooled almost any doctor when
the victim was alive, although the large bone-structure,
and especially the big hands and feet and the pronounced

Adam's apple might have given rise to comment. I'll send you a full report in the morning.'

'You've given me quite a shock, Peláez. Perhaps the murderer had a shock too. Could that explain the vicious wound in the genitals?'

'Possibly, since there was no apparent sexual assault on the first two victims, who were genuinely female. I'm sending the clothes round to Varga's lab in sealed plastic bags. I'll also take a photograph of the face without the cosmetics and with the hair masked. That will give you a better idea of how the victim looked as a man.'

'Thanks for letting me know so quickly, Peláez.'

Bernal sat down and took out his packet of Kaiser, offering them to Navarro and Gallardo. 'That's a new poser for us. The girl found at Concepción was an emasculated man, dressed up as a woman. A transsexual. Peláez says he could have passed for a woman under almost any medical examination. Have the photos been brought up yet, Paco?'

'Yes, *jefe*, but they're still a bit damp.'

'Let's have a look at the victim again.' Bernal pulled out one of the close-ups of the face. 'That one's usable. She or he doesn't look too dead on that, apart from the bloodstains on the chin. Order more of that number from Photography for them to do by the morning, Paco. Now Ángel, give us the low-down on the *travestís*.' Bernal knew that Ángel Gallardo would have a pretty good idea of the transvestite night-clubs and bars, since he had worked undercover in the city's constantly changing vice scene.

'Well, I'll have to check with the Anti-Vice Group's records, but there seem to be three classes of establishment. The three or four up-market cabarets, which specialize in transvestite shows, rely on established artistes, often visiting international ones. It's not thought many of that type of artiste "have had the operation", as they put it. Then there are the smaller, more discreet, *boîtes*, which often take on amateur talent. You'd be surprised to know that some of their artistes, who nearly always perform in playback—miming to records of famous singers—are often respectable bank clerks or insurance agents in the daytime, but their own mothers wouldn't recognize them with the wigs, gowns and make-up they wear at night. It may be that a few genuine trans-sexuals get taken on in those clubs. Finally there are the seedier basement bars where the transvestites meet for a drink in the small hours, when they summon up the courage to dress up and slip out of their houses under the noses of their neighbours. It's quite a busy scene, really, although the general public fortunately sees little of it, except those who frequent the posh cabarets.'

Bernal sighed heavily. 'It's going to take a lot of men to ask questions in all the places you mention. How many such establishments do you think there are?'

'Anti-Vice could give us the latest list, but in the whole city there are probably twelve to fifteen, counting the small bars where they sometimes hang out, but some have been closed down.'

'Could you make a start tonight, and show this photograph around? We've got to identify the victim quickly if we can. Do you want someone to accompany you?' He looked nervously at Navarro. Bernal hated *boîtes* and discothèques and hoped he wouldn't have to volunteer.

'No, I don't think so. You, *jefe*, and Paco look too official, if you know what I mean.'

'You mean they'll think I'm the late Caudillo, come to close them down?' Bernal often joked openly about his resemblance to the late dictator, which had sometimes proved useful when questioning the more neurotic among the suspects.

'No, it's not that so much, chief.' Ángel hesitated. 'You

two don't really look like the usual sort of client of those places.'

'You think we're too old and square-looking, is that it?' asked Navarro.

'Something like that. Now Elena, she'd be good. Excellent cover, in fact. Actress types often go into the clubs with their admirers after their shows.'

'Her father would never forgive me if I sent her to such places,' said Bernal. 'She'd better stick to the old-clothes dealers for the moment.'

RETIRO

Bernal downed his second Larios *gin tonic* in Félix Pérez's bar and waved good-night to the barman. Out in the cool night, he was suddenly engulfed by a gang of youths wearing blue shirts, who were shouting '*¡Viva Franco!*' and giving the extended-arm salute as they weaved their way between the pedestrians. As he stood back in the doorway of a television shop on the corner of the Calle de Lagasca, he noticed that some of them were armed with bicycle-chains and baseball bats. From a distance, below the Puerta de Alcalá, came the sound of a large crowd singing the Internationale, and he glimpsed far-off red banners. Another confrontation! Nearly every night now, as election day approached, there were clashes in the central districts. The socialists and communists came up from Vallecas and Delicias and gathered at Atocha, while the fascists assembled in the Salamanca quarter, mainly in the Calle de Goya, and sallied forth in sudden razzias. As he turned into his street, four jeeps of the Anti-disturbios raced down Alcalá with sirens screaming, followed by a grey minibus with wire-covered windows, which was packed with riot police armed with tear-gas launchers and rifles loaded, he hoped, with rubber bullets. Raised over their heads were plastic riot-visors, which made them look as though they were on their way to outer space, but underneath the helmets he caught a glimpse of the very young and rather frightened peasant faces, lips puffing on a last, nervous cigarette.

In the doorway of his house, Bernal found the portress peeping anxiously out.

'Oh, Superintendent, how lucky it's you! Is there rioting? Oh, what a saint we've lost in the Caudillo! Spain will be ruined by all this politicking.'

'Don't worry, señora, the riot police have just arrived. They'll try to keep the two sides apart.'

His private view was that in earlier clashes they had made things worse, by provoking the populace. He himself had nearly got gassed by them on the Gran Vía a week earlier, and had had to take refuge in the Cafetería Zahara.

Upstairs he discovered Eugenia crouching behind her potted plants, peering through the railings of the terrace at the disorder down the street.

'Oh, Luis,' she moaned, 'I knew it! It's going to be 1936 all over again!'

ANTÓN MARTÍN

That same evening, as she slogged along the Calle de San Sebastián, Inspectora Elena Fernández felt that she was gradually learning the wearisome and frustrating business of detection. She had already interviewed seven dealers in old clothes, and the peculiar smell of their wares clung in her nostrils. She was now on the track of Señora Aurora, who, she had been assured, would be tucking down for the night in the portals of the Church of St Sebastian.

Turning into the upper part of the Calle de Atocha, she saw the massive portico of the church with its high wrought-iron grilles, which seemed to be firmly locked. She peered uncertainly through the railings, and at first could make out nothing in the gathering darkness. Then, as her eyes grew inured to the penumbra, she glimpsed the moving whiteness of a pair of hands.

'Señora,' she called. *'¿Es usted Señora Aurora?'*

'Who wants her?' came the reply, almost in a cackle.

'I want to see you about some old clothes.'

'Well, you can't get in this way. You'll have to go round to the small gate at the side.'

Elena retraced her steps and found she had earlier passed a small iron gate without noticing it. Inside the high, open-sided portico, she strained her eyes in the gloom and just made out what appeared to be a pile of rags on the steps. Getting closer, she saw a figure dressed in black, surrounded by battered suitcases and cardboard boxes stuffed with items of clothing. The gnarled hands were cutting up an apple.

'Señora Aurora?' she enquired tentatively.

'What do you want, a well-dressed girl like you? You don't need any of these rags.'

'No, señora, but I'm looking for a gentleman who may have bought a lot of clothes from you, either bit by bit, or all at once.'

'What did he look like?'

'I've got a picture of him here you could look at, but it's rather dark for you to see it.' Elena wished she'd brought a torch.

The old woman took the picture and shuffled towards the street to see it under the street-light. 'Never seen him,' she said. 'Could be anyone with such a beard.'

'What about this one, then?' asked Elena, producing the other Photofit picture of the suspect, when he was clean-shaven.

'Pretty ordinary-looking. Not a good photo, is it?' said Señora Aurora. 'But then my eyes are not as good as they were. Why are you looking for these two men? You from the police?' Elena remembered Bernal's warning that in this area they wouldn't give one another away to the authorities.

'They're not really photos, just a kind of drawing. It's just that my mother sold them some old clothes, and she included a valuable dress by mistake, which she wants to get back.' Elena thought this sounded pretty feeble, especially if the old woman asked why they'd gone to the bother of obtaining pictures of the supposed dealers, or why they were alleged to have bought clothes from her, rather than sell some to her.

'Never seen either of them at my pitch. Anyway, business is not like it used to be. Most people earn too much these days to want second-hand clothes. They go off to the Galerías Preciados and spend it all on new ones, which they only wear for five minutes. You'd be amazed at the quality of the stuff they throw out, but there's no shifting it now.' She went morosely back to her apple.

Elena wondered if she should give her alms, since she was so poor, and she fished in her bag for a hundred-peseta note. 'Well, thank you, señora. God be with you.'

'Go with God, señorita,' replied the old woman, tucking the banknote into her corsage with a very expert movement.

Elena decided to call it a day, and set off wearily down the Calle de Atocha to catch the Microbús 6 to her home in El Viso. Far down the street, in the main square, she could see a procession of red banners and could hear the rhythmic chanting of '¡Es-pa-ña! ¡Ma-ña-na! ¡Se-rá re-pu-bli-ca-na!' She pulled her coat more tightly round her shoulders.

JOSÉ ANTONIO

At 9.30 p.m., Ángel Gallardo was consulting his long list of current girl-friends and debating on which to ring up. Teresa, perhaps? She'd enjoy visiting those night-clubs. Or Mercedes? She looks more the part, especially if she wears her blue leather outfit. I'll try her first.

He'd always managed to be surrounded by adoring females, who would visit his small studio flat in the Calle de Tres Cruces, in the very centre of Madrid, and do his washing and ironing, as well as console him in other ways. They thought him the wittiest and most *enterado* or knowledgeable escort they'd ever had.

He put down his Braun electric razor and picked up the phone. 'Merché? That you? Want a fling tonight round the *travestí* bars? Be fun, eh?' There was a pause. 'You can't? Really?' Ángel was flabbergasted, especially when Mercedes went on to reveal that she was involved in a UCD party meeting that night.

After five more unsuccessful calls, he began to think that all the *madrileñas* had deserted sex for politics. Finally, in some desperation, he rang Inspectora Elena Fernández at her home, despite Bernal's vetoing of the idea that she should be involved in this part of the investigation.

'Elena? This is Ángel. I've drawn a blank with all my girl-friends in finding an escort for tonight to visit the bars the *jefe* wants.' Elena chortled with amusement. 'It's true, honestly. They've taken up politics all of a sudden.'

'Wise kids,' said Elena drily. 'I hope they're doing it for the right party.'

'Which one's that, do you think?'

'You're not going to catch me out like that, Ángel.' Elena weighed up the matter quickly. She was slightly worried that he might try to take advantage of her, and he had admitted that Bernal had expressly forbidden it.

On the other hand, it was a marvellous chance to see underground Madrid, rather than just the Madrid Underground. 'All right then, Ángel. Where will you meet me?'

Ángel couldn't believe his ears, or his luck. 'We'll have dinner in a posh restaurant first, if you like. How about La Barraca, in the Calle de la Reina? It's just behind the Gran Vía below the Telefónica.'

'Very well. I know where it is.'

'Don't forget to put on your kinkiest outfit.'

Elena pretended to ignore this remark. 'I'll take a taxi and I'll see you there at 9.45.'

Two hours later, replete from a large Valencian paella and a bottle of Marqués de Riscal Special Reserve, Ángel and Elena set out on a round of the clubs to the north of the Gran Vía. He thought she had got her outfit exactly right: a slim-fitting black dress with a long red fringe around the bodice and hem, over black patent-leather three-quarter boots. He had finally decided to wear a leather bomber-jacket over an open-necked Christian Dior shirt and tight black trousers. They both looked sufficiently *progre* or 'with it', he considered; almost enough to dance a *sevillana* in the middle of Callao Square.

TRIBUNAL

The first club they visited was near the Church of St Ildefonso, and it was called El Satiro—'The Satyr'. Despite it's unobtrusive entrance, it opened out into a surprisingly large cellar, done out in someone's idea of Art Déco. In the dim ultra-violet light, they could make out five or six young people dancing to very loud rock music on the minuscule dance-floor; from their elegant clothes, their peacock-like postures and their blank lack of recognition of one another's existence, it was clear that they rated themselves as belonging to a latter-day *jeunesse dorée*. In front of the bar, two strangely dressed waiters balanced trays of *gin tonics*, San Franciscos, and whiskies with Coke, and argued with the older of the two barmen.

Ángel led Elena to the high stools at the far corner, where they were confronted by a surly young barman, who was clearly also acting as disc-jockey. When Elena was comfortably arranged on a high stool, whence she could survey the other clients, Ángel greeted the young barman like a long-lost friend, and ordered two Johnnie Walker's Black Label, mentally recording the outrageous charge of 700 pesetas to add to his expenses sheet. After chatting for a while about various *travestís* with whom they appeared to have common acquaintance, Ángel showed the barman the photograph of the unidentified corpse.

'She's in the hospital where I work, and she's suffering from temporary amnesia,' he said, 'so we're trying to find someone who knows her, you see.'

'Well, with all that blood on her chin and her eyes shut, she's hard to identify. What happened to her?'

'Oh, a street accident. She crossed on a green light and the bus driver paid no attention. You know how they drive in this city,' said Ángel airily. 'The other doctors and I would be happier if we knew who she was.' Ángel rather fancied himself in the role of junior houseman, with all the opportunities to tickle the young nurses in the laundry cupboards.

'It's possible she's been in here once or twice,' said the barman, 'but she didn't look like that. I'll just show it to Eduardo. He's worked here longer than me.'

Eduardo left his altercation with the waiters and approached Ángel and Elena suspiciously. 'Been in an accident, you say?'

'Yes, she's in La Paz Clinic, where I work as a houseman,' said Ángel, warming to the role.

'She may have been in here as a customer,' admitted Eduardo, 'but she's never worked as a performer in the floor show. You two going to stay for that?'

'Oh, I expect so,' said Ángel, 'considering what you charge for the whisky.'

'That's meant to include the shows. The second one that starts at 2 a.m. is more daring than the first.'

'We'll probably stay for both, won't we, Elena?'

'Depends how good the girls are in the first one,' she said, placing a king-size cigarette in an immensely long, silver and ebony holder, which she allowed Eduardo to light for her. She smiled at him knowingly through the first emission of smoke, which glowed exaggeratedly like his frilled shirt front under the ultraviolet lights.

'You recall what name she went by when she used to come here?' asked Ángel casually, anxious to bring the conversation back to the photograph of the murdered trans-sexual.

'I think I heard the others call her Carla, or Carol, or some name like that. About a year ago she asked the boss for a job in the show. He thought she was too skinny, but I suppose she could have dressed up as Shirley Bassey. He's over at the other club tonight, near Ópera, but he'll be in for the second show.'

'Do you mean all the artistes imitate famous singers?' asked Elena.

'Oh yes, in playback. Some of them are better than the originals, believe me. We see them all here, even the dead ones. Édith Piaf, Marilyn Monroe, you name them, we get them. These *travestís* nearly always have a fixation on one particular star; then they go to their films or study their photos, and listen to their records again and again till they get every detail right. It's amazing how realistically they can do it.'

'And this Carol or Carla, who did she imitate?'

'Well, if it's the same one, no one I could think of. That's why the boss didn't take her on, I think. She'd have to get into the big league to appear just as herself.'

Elena and Ángel witnessed the first few numbers of the show, which began with a grand parade of the whole cast of seven, dressed in flamenco *trajes de cola* — flounced and sequined skirts, and high combs with black mantillas. But then, taking advantage of the semi-darkness offered by an unconvincing Édith Piaf, they skipped up the stairs, where Ángel tipped the doorman who let them out into the silent square in front of the Church of St Ildefonso.

'We'll get a taxi just around the corner in Fuencarral,' said Ángel, putting Elena's red Manila shawl over her shoulders. 'I hope you've got the stamina for a few more of these places.'

'They're quite fun, really, Ángel, especially to see how the *travestís*, by imitating female mannerisms, so overdo it that they never look convincing. They're really a separate breed, aren't they?'

'It must be their chromosomes,' said Ángel laconically.

ÓPERA

The second club, which came under the same management, was in an alley off the Plaza de Isabel II, commonly known as Ópera. It was an older and seedier establishment, called 'Unisex'.

'This is more how I expected it to be,' whispered Elena nervously, as they fought their way through the packed front bar and passed lines of *chulos* who leaned nonchalantly against the walls, looking as though they'd slit their grandmothers' throats for tuppence, she thought.

Beyond a beaded curtain they glimpsed the inner cabaret, where two long rows of candlelit tables were arranged on each side of an aisle, where the first show was clearly reaching its finale. The scratched gramophone record of Lola Flores was excessively amplified, and the large transvestite miming to the voice of the famous artiste was making such exaggerated gestures that they seemed disconnected with the music and with herself.

Ángel led Elena to two empty seats near the beaded curtain.

'What'll you have?' asked a waiter, dressed in black bell-bottomed trousers as tight as those of the dancer Antonio.

'*Dos güisquis con hielo.* Better make them Black Label,' said Ángel, though he thought it probable that all the spirits would be falsified, whatever the label said.

Tumultuous applause greeted the end of the false Lola Flores turn, and the performer was clearly well known to the regulars, who shouted '¡*Olé!*' and '¡*Bis, bis!*' to try and get a repeat of the number.

'Don't worry, señores,' said the smooth compère through his crackling microphone, 'you'll see plenty of La Pastora del Monte later on.'

'Looked a bit hefty to be a "hill shepherdess", don't you think?' whispered Elena, giggling at the *nom de théâtre*.

'I'll tell you what he looks like without the wig when I come back,' answered Ángel. 'I'm going behind the scenes to see the manager. Don't let anybody rape you, Elena, while I'm away.'

'Fat chance of that.'

She sipped her whisky calmly for a while, listening to the loud chatter over the amplified voice of Donna Summers, when she became disconcertedly aware of a large dishevelled woman opposite, enveloped in a sack-like dress, winking at her. The woman held her head at an odd angle, and waved her empty glass dreamily in the air, demanding more whisky of the passing waiters, who studiously ignored her. As she squatted on the padded velvet stool, under a reproduction of an Alphonse Mucha poster, the middle-aged woman continued to make futile half-gestures, as though trying to harangue an audience, and to grimace knowingly at Elena, who despite her strong inclination to look the other way, was transfixed by the sight of her.

'Now, now, no more for you, you've had enough,' said an older waiter to the woman, who seemed more than inebriated.'Why don't you go home, *querida?*'

The woman began to gesture more violently, but almost speechlessly, then she suddenly slumped forward, and Elena watched in horrified amazement as water began to pour round the red plush stool on which the woman sat, until it formed a miniature lake of urine surrounding the mountainous figure of the micturitrix.

'That's it! Now you've done it! Out with you!' and two waiters lifted the offender bodily to the side door, where she could be heard protesting still.

'Drugs, that's what gets them,' said the other waiter to Elena, who was quite shaken by the scene. 'They mix it with the drink, and it knocks 'em out.'

SOL

At 8.30 the next morning, which was Saturday, 11 June, Navarro chatted to Peláez in the bar opposite the DGS office as the pathologist sipped a *sol y sombra* — in its Madrid form, an anisette with brandy.

'The Superintendent will be at the office in about a quarter of an hour, doctor,' said Paco. 'He sounded out of breath when I rang to tell him you were bringing the report on the *travesti.*'

'More than that, I've brought you the fingerprints and a cast and photographs of the dentition to help with the ID.'

As they talked, Navarro listened in occasionally to the conversation of the other customers with the barman. One businessman brandished a copy of *Ya*, and remarked that his wife was afraid to travel on the Metro any more. 'It's costing me a fortune in taxis, I can tell you. When will they capture this maniac, eh?'

Navarro had noticed that *Ya*, *El País* and *ABC*, the serious dailies, had played down the Metro murders. In any case their pages were loaded with the political meetings taking place prior to the first general elections to be held since February 1936. But the three murders reported so far, despite the lack of detailed reports, had gripped the minds of the Madrid public as a sort of diversion from politics. He hadn't seen signs of real panic, but he knew from his wife's reaction that women had a real unspoken fear of the psychopath, whom they invested with the worst features of their most horrific nightmares.

RETIRO

No such apprehensions were to be observed in Eugenia Carrero de Bernal that morning as she directed her husband Luis and her son Diego to up-end the iron-framed piano with the faded rosewood veneer in the hallway of the flat, in order to manœuvre it along the corridor to the dining-room.

'Watch out for the radiator outside the bathroom door, Luis. Don't let it scrape against the terrace door, Diego.'

'I don't think it will get through the passage doorway, Geñita,' protested Bernal.

'It will, now you've taken the door off its hinges,' said

Navarro waiting for him.

'Has Ángel rung in?'

'Not yet, *jefe*, but it's a bit early for him.'

'Well, Peláez, have you found the cause of death?'

'I think it could have been an alkaloid poison — cocaine or an opiate — but the toxicologist will have to test the organs for it. There was no disease, and the only physical injuries consisted of the stabbing in the genital area, and two injection marks, one in the left arm and one in the back of the left hand. Strange, that. Wonder if he was given a sort of pre-med. with Pentothal? I've asked the Institute to check for it. The reconstructed female genitals were stabbed a number of times with a curiously shaped instrument — something like a spoon, perhaps, but with flatter edges. Can't think what it was, exactly. Anyway, I've brought you the fingerprints and a cast of the dentition. No dentures, but a number of fillings. And what may help you, a recent filling in the upper right second premolar; the common, cheap silver alloy was used. Skilfully done. It's recent, because the metal is still bright and slightly soft. There are eight older fillings, two of porcelain at the front, and there are two extractions. Only two of the third molars have erupted, one left upper and one right lower; the other two were impacted.'

'Would the impacted wisdom teeth have given him pain?' asked Bernal.

'Hard to tell; there was little sign of periodontitis. But it's worth mentioning if you're going to enquire of all the dentists. You've got good casts here which they may well identify, especially since some dentist will have seen him or her recently, no doubt in his female manifestation.'

'I'll put Miranda and Lista on it at once. Paco, send the fingerprints to Criminal Records first, with a copy to the Documento Nacional de Identidad. It would take them many days, if not weeks, of course, to track down the right index-finger and thumb prints in the complete national files, but it may be the only way. After all, the dental work may not have been done in Madrid at all, and even if it were, there are hundreds of dentists to check. What about the blood group, Peláez?'

'I sent samples to the hæmatologist yesterday. I told him to let you know this morning, as soon as the preliminary tests are complete. That way you'll know if the blood placed in the sacs in the earlier victims' mouths is the same as in this victim.'

'What do you make of the genital injury in psychological terms, Peláez? Do you think the murderer attacked this victim sexually?'

'Not when the trans-sexual was alive, because the wound was *post mortem*, and there were no semen traces. Unless he's turned to necrophiliac practices, it may demonstrate his rage at discovering, or suspecting, that the supposed girl was an operated man.'

'One thing that puzzles me, chief,' said Navarro, 'is how someone like this victim gets a job and earns enough to live on. Who would employ such a person?'

'That's an interesting question,' said Peláez. 'I examined the cadaver for occupational marks or deformations. You both know that the hands often give a clue to occupation, but this person's are free from callouses and are well manicured. That gives us some information. Secondly, the feet: he or she didn't do much walking in any employment. Thirdly, the spine shows no sign of curvature, nor are the shoulders bowed, so there's no suggestion of a sedentary job. Really, there's only negative evidence that the victim didn't do any of these things on a long-term basis.'

'And what was the approximate age?' Bernal enquired.

'Early twenties, I should say.'

'Can you fix the time of death more precisely?'

'The stomach showed a practically digested breakfast of coffee and *churros* or *porras* — some pancake mixture cooked in olive oil, at any rate. But, as I said earlier, it's the one meal that hardly helps to pinpoint the time more precisely. I can only suggest a time of decease between 9.30 and 11 a.m., and that's really based on the temperature and the start of rigor. I'm sorry I can't be more helpful on this one, but it's a fascinating case. It'll certainly figure in my memoirs!'

Soon after Peláez's departure, Elena came in, dressed elegantly in a light tweed suit, and she greeted Bernal and Navarro. She reported on her questioning of the old-clothes dealers the previous day, but said nothing about her nocturnal escapade with Ángel, as they had agreed.

'Perhaps you'll have more luck tomorrow at the Rastro,' Bernal consoled her.

Ángel arrived late as usual, with his customary jauntiness, but with tell-tale rings under his eyes. 'What a night, oh, what a night we had!' He rolled his eyes suggestively at Navarro, while deliberately averting them from Elena, who was studiously examining a report at her desk.

'Come on then,' said Bernal impatiently, 'There's no need to go into all the gory details. Did you get a lead on the dead transvestite?'

'Only that two people thought they recognized the photo as being of a person called Carol. I've arranged to meet some former friends of hers tonight, thanks to the manager of the Club Unisex.'

'Carol,' mused Bernal. 'That's just a nickname, I suppose. Do you think it was based on his real name? Perhaps his christian name was Carlos?'

'It's possible,' conceded Ángel, 'but from what I've heard it's more likely it was taken from some famous star of the past. They often seem to call themselves "Gloria", "Marilyn", "Josephine", "Lola" and so on. Perhaps this one named himself after Carole Lombard.'

'Did you get any information about where they get

the operation done?'

'Hardly any of them have been able to afford it, but they all say they'd have to go to Morocco.'

'Did you get any impression of drug-taking among them?' asked Navarro.

'It's mainly "alc", but I gathered they sometimes smoke hash and take a few "poppers" when they can get them.'

'What are they, Ángel?' asked Elena curiously.

'Capsules of amyl nitrate, which they sniff for a quick boost.'

'But no narcotics?' asked Bernal.

'They didn't mention anything stronger.'

After Miranda and Lista had arrived, Bernal gave them all a summary of the pathologist's initial findings. 'Of course, we have to wait for detailed reports from the toxicologist and the hæmatologist which we'll get on Monday. At present Varga is going over the victim's clothes. As you will realize, the most urgent task is to identify him. I suggest that we all concentrate this morning on the dentists. Paco will split up the total list between us by district. We've got copies of the photograph of the dental cast Peláez has taken. Most of them work on Saturday mornings, but only until one o'clock or so. If any of you gets a possible identification you should ring through to Paco at once. Ángel, you will see the alleged friends of this "Carol" tonight, and you can ring me at home tomorrow to report. Juan, you could accompany Elena to the Rastro tomorrow morning, to complete the questioning of the rag-merchants. We'll all meet back here on Monday morning at 9 a.m. Agreed?'

After dividing up the list of dentists into five areas, Navarro handed the first four sections to the four inspectors, who then departed.

'I'll do this last section, chief, if you'll keep watch in the office. It'll do me good to get some fresh air, and it's a sunny morning.'

'That's good of you, Paco. I'll take the opportunity to dictate a preliminary report for the examining magistrate.'

CHUECA

When the green underground train on Line 5 left José Antonio station, Matilde Gómez looked at the long package on the floor at the end of the carriage with some puzzlement. Earlier she had assumed that it belonged to one of the men who had been standing inside the rear door. But now the carriage was nearly empty, and the parcel had clearly been forgotten. She looked at the older lady sitting diagonally opposite her, and smiled. 'Someone's left it behind, I think,' said Matilde, indicating the brown-paper parcel neatly tied with string.

'I hope it's not an ETA bomb,' commented the well-dressed lady, nervously clicking a black, lace-edged fan open and shut. 'With so much going on these days, one's almost afraid to go out of doors.'

'And those terrible murders,' exclaimed Matilde. 'They don't seem able to put a stop to them. Perhaps we should tell the guard,' she suggested, as the train drew into Chueca station. 'Look, there's a policeman on the platform. Shall we call him?'

'Perhaps we should,' agreed the older lady.

At Matilde's urgent beckoning, the grey-uniformed *guardia* looked into the carriage and he whistled to the guard. 'Hold the train! There's something to see to here.'

SERRANO

That same Saturday morning a similar scene occurred at Serrano station on Line 4. A policeman heard a woman calling him as the train doors opened.

'*¡Guardia! ¡Señor Guardia! ¡Venga aquí, por favor!*' An old lady was pointing to a long package propped up in the corner of the carriage. 'It smells peculiar,' she almost whispered to him. The *gris* had the train halted and removed the package to the station-master's office.

SOL

Bernal was half way through the dictation of his report to the Juzgado de Guardia when the head of Metro Security rang him.

'A package has been discovered on a train at Chueca station, Superintendent. Its contents are gruesome in the extreme. It appears to be a human limb, in an advanced state of putrefaction.'

'Try to get them to handle the wrappings as little as possible,' said Bernal calmly. 'There may be fingerprints. Who is in charge there?'

'They've called Inspector Lara from Chamberí district police-station.'

'I'll ring through to him and get him to take the package to Peláez's laboratory. Is there a witness?'

'A woman called Matilde Gómez, a servant. She's making a statement for Inspector Lara.'

'Very well. We'll keep in touch.'

Bernal looked at the large plan of the Metro which adorned the wall of the outer office. Chueca was on Line 5, the line that had only been completed in 1970. If this latest find originated from the Metro murderer, he had not only turned to dismemberment of his victims, but also there was no rhyme or reason in his movements.

By lunch-time Bernal was close to despair. He had rung Peláez to ask him to stand by to examine the human limb when the first report came in from Metro Security.

Now, five such parcels had been found at five different Metro stations, none of which was even on the same line. All the discoveries were being taken to the Instituto Anatómico Forense, and Bernal had warned Prieto of Fingerprints that there would be a lot of wrapping paper to examine that afternoon. None of his detectives had telephoned with any information from the dentists.

At 1.30 Navarro arrived and slumped into his chair. 'I've done a quarter of my list, *jefe*, and none of the dentists recognized the dentition as belonging to one of his patients, nor the fillings as his work.'

'I've got worse news, Paco. Five dismembered pieces of human remains wrapped in paper parcels have been discovered in different trains on the Metro this morning.' Bernal pointed at the map. 'I've put in brown flags to mark the stations. You can see it's quite arbitrary. If it's our man, he's distributing the pieces like confetti.'

'Good God!' exclaimed Navarro. 'Do you think he's cut up the corpse of the victim from whom he extracted the blood of the B negative group?'

'In one way, I hope so, Paco. Then, at least, there won't have been a fifth victim. Peláez and the hæmatologist should be able to tell us.'

Shortly afterwards the pathologist telephoned. 'So far, Bernal, I've got a left leg amputated at the knee and ankle, but no left foot, and a right arm from shoulder to wrist.'

'There are three more packages on their way to you, Peláez.'

'Let's hope one of them contains the sacrum or one of the hip-bones. Otherwise it will be difficult to tell the sex of the victim, let alone the age. Decomposition is advanced in the two limbs I've got, but there is no insect infestation. A very curious feature: there are signs of formation of adipocere, which is very rare.'

'What does that imply, Peláez?' asked Bernal.

'Well, what it means is that the body fat is turning into a whitish, wax-like substance. Now this only occurs when the cadaver is left in very damp, cool conditions, and it doesn't take place for six to eight weeks. If the Metro murderer is responsible, it suggests that these remains belong to his earliest known victim.'

'What about the blood group?'

'I'm sending samples over to the hæmatologist, but you will realize that the blood is entirely congealed and deteriorated. Still, he should be able to test for the ABO groups, and the MN, Gm(a) and Hp factors from the dried samples. We may then be able to compare it with the blood-print we have from the blood found in the plastic sacs forced into the mouths of the three other victims.'

'I'm sorry I'm giving you a busy weekend, Peláez.'

'Glad to be of service. You've got a very inventive criminal to find. By the way, I forgot to tell you he seems to have studied anatomy. The dismemberment was quite expertly done, with a surgical saw.'

'You don't think it's one of your colleagues, gone over the edge at last?'

'Ha!' said Peláez. 'Wouldn't be a bit surprised. None of us is normal, you know. I'll be back to you when I've seen more of this cadaver. Hope the bits all fit.'

'I hope so too, Peláez. *Hasta luego*.'

Bernal gave Navarro a summary of Peláez's initial report on the two limbs. 'We'd better take it in turns to have lunch, in order to keep the office manned. Will you draw up a rota for the rest of the weekend?'

RETIRO

By the time Bernal sat down that night to a supper of greasy veal chops with a hunk of almost cold left-overs' omelette, Eugenia's evening speciality, he knew that Peláez had less than a third of one human cadaver, which was possibly that of a woman in her twenties, but no head, torso or hands had yet been found — the very parts which would help in identification.

Eugenia ended her protracted grace in which he was supposed to utter the responses, and she switched on the television.

'Bring some of that wine from your province, Geñita. Where's Diego?'

'He went out with some of his friends from the Faculty an hour ago. I wish he wouldn't stay out so late every night. You shouldn't give him so much pocket-money.'

'He's got to find out about the world, Geñita. He'd be worse in the long run if we kept him in.'

'He doesn't need to find out the world's a bad place,' she muttered. 'He's been taught that since he was a child.'

'More's the pity,' said Luis, pouring himself a large glassful of the red wine, which Eugenia had brought from her village. 'Youth should keep its illusions for as long as possible.'

Eugenia pointedly turned up the TV sound, and the *Telediario* began with a long election report. Bernal pricked up his ears when the Madrid Metro was mentioned.

'Mysterious packages were discovered in a number of Metro trains this morning. It is understood that they may be related to the recently found murder victims. Superintendent Bernal and his group of the Brigada Criminal are investigating.'

'They mentioned you, Luis,' exclaimed Eugenia. 'Oh, how shameful! I do hope my family in Ciudad Rodrigo weren't watching!'

'The only shameful thing about it is that I can't catch the criminal who's perpetrating these foul crimes,' said Bernal. 'Detection is an honourable profession.'

'But so squalid, Luis. Just think of the kind of people you have to question! Prostitutes and the like. My father wanted you to take up farming, you know.'

Bernal groaned at this piece of ancient history, and dug savagely into a rather burnt veal chop.

LA LATINA

Inspectora Elena Fernández, dressed in a smart Sunday-morning outfit (she had earlier accompanied her mother to the seven o'clock Mass), stood at the entrance to La Latina underground station in the Plaza de la Cebada, waiting for her colleague Juan Lista. She had cheated a little by taking a taxi, instead of travelling on Line 5 from Rubén Darío, but felt fresher for it. Indeed, although she wouldn't confess to it, the recent events had given her a distaste for Metro travel, which she had never relished at the best of times.

At that hour of the morning, just before nine, she noticed a large number of people crossing the Calle de Toledo, making for the rag-fair at the Rastro. There were also last-minute traders, with their families helping them to carry their wares to their particular pitches. Soon Juan Lista came up the Metro steps and greeted her.

'You're looking ravishing today, Elena. I hope your clothes don't get crushed in the crowd we're going to have to fight our way through.'

'I had to go to church with my mother first. Where do you think most of the old-clothes dealers will be?'

'Many of them will be in that narrow side-street that runs off the Ribera de Curtidores. Mira el Río Alta, I think it's called.'

'I haven't been here since my father used to bring me when I was small,' said Elena nostalgically. 'I remember it seemed like a wonderland to a child, full of fascinating gewgaws.'

'Well, they say there's nothing you could want that you couldn't find in the Rastro—at a price. But the tourists have ruined the bargains one used to be able to find in the antiques line.'

'I didn't know you were interested in antiques, Juan.'

'I've only got a few brasses and some old pocket-watches and fob-chains. I was starting a collection, but they've got priced beyond my means these days.'

They could already hear the cries of the street-vendors as they walked along the Calle de las Maldonadas, and their ears were assailed by noise as they entered the Plaza de Cascorro, which was dominated by the statue of Eloy Gonzalo, the Madrid soldier who, with a lighted can of petrol, drove out the Cuban insurrectionists from the village of Cascorro in Camagüey to bring them to battle with the Spanish troops.

Elena realized that most of the shouting she could hear came from the tables set up by the political parties, where passers-by were offered propaganda, boxes of matches, cheap lighters, key-rings, and even wrapped sweets, all bearing the party's symbol. Gazing down the steep Ribera de Curtidores—'the Slope of the Leather-tanners'—where the stalls loaded with goods sparkled in the warm sunshine, she was taken aback by the thick, slowly moving snakes of people, passing up and down between the vendors.

Lista tried to part the crowds for her as they fought their way a few hundred metres down the hill. Elena stopped to look at the very old man carving objects out of bone, and spotted the ornate notice which proclaimed that he had carved ivory buttons 'by appointment to Queen Victoria Eugenia'.

When they found the street they were seeking, the going was somewhat easier, and they glanced with interest at the open shop-fronts displaying horse-brasses, cow-bells and other rustic implements, and they said good-morning to a bright-eyed old woman who super-intended an enormous pile of crystal droppers of all kinds, taken, Elena assumed, from hundreds of chandeliers and candelabra of the last century.

'*¡Lágrimas! ¡Lágrimas de todo tipo!*' cried the old woman. 'Tears' they were called, Elena remembered.

'I'll cry one for you, if you can't find the "tear" you want in this pile,' joked the woman to the crowd.

When Elena and Juan found the first old-clothes dealer, a heavy shower suddenly soaked the dense crowd, and they took refuge in the doorway of a shop.

'I'll buy you an umbrella, Elena,' said Juan. 'They say you can find anything here.'

After a tiring morning, dodging the frequent showers, they had interviewed eleven clothes-dealers and rag-merchants without any of them recognizing the Photofit pictures of the suspect.

ATOCHA

Bernal, meanwhile, had been called to the Instituto Anatómico Forense by Dr Peláez, who had made a partial reconstruction of the dismembered corpse.

'As you can see, Bernal, most of her is still missing. I think the remains are female, but I cannot be certain until you find the pelvis.'

'All these parts belong to the same body?'

'Yes, I'm fairly sure. I've done all the usual bone-measurement tests, and the hæmatologist should be able to confirm it when he checks the blood groups.'

'Any way of identifying the cadaver, Peláez?'

'Yes, I'm hopeful. One of the other three packages contained the right hand, but the skin had been removed from the fingertips, presumably in an attempt to prevent identification. However, I'm trying to take dermal prints by soaking the fingers in formalin and then photographing them at an oblique angle under a strong light. The whorls, loops and deltas extend into the flesh, of course, and are not confined to the epidermis — something the murderer did not know.'

'Then the right hand is by far the more useful, because we'll get the DNI to check the right index-finger and thumb prints in their files, if there's nothing in the criminal ones.'

'It's a pity we haven't got the head,' said Peláez, 'then you could have the dentition.'

'Oh, the prints will be good enough, if you can take them successfully.'

As he watched Peláez's skilful work, Bernal turned away from the putrid limbs on the slab, his stomach churning as usual when he was in the mortuary.

Peláez, knowing his colleague's queasiness, said without looking up from his task: 'Wait for me in my office, Luis. My secretary will bring you some coffee.'

Bernal went gratefully. Lighting up a Kaiser, he pondered on the psychopath, of whom he still didn't have a clear mental picture. They now knew that he had some anatomical knowledge. Had he trained as a doctor or for some other related profession which required a study of anatomy? Why was he luring young girls and cruelly murdering them? Above all, why the plastic bags in the mouths, and the disposal of the bodies in the Metro? Bernal knew he was committing the error of trying to think logically about a person who performed quite illogical acts, but he remembered having come across somewhere the phrase 'the logic of madness'. Within the bounds of his madness, was the psychopath behaving in a way that seemed logical to him? Certainly, there had been a pattern at first, now broken if the dismembered corpse was one of his deeds. Earlier, it had seemed that he wanted, almost like a *metteur en scène*, to create a series of similar images, really the *same* image, of a girl dead in a Metro train, with blood pouring from her mouth. That sequence had begun with the dolls, then had continued with the two murdered girls. The dead trans-sexual had spoilt the image, perhaps to the psychopath's fury, which would explain the savage genital injury in that case. That event had, perhaps, led to the dismemberment. But who was this victim? The first one, whose blood the killer had used for the sac-in-the-mouth effect in the other cases? Bernal decided to put the whole theory to Peláez, who now emerged triumphant.

'It was tricky, but I think I've got sufficiently good photos of dermal prints for Prieto to check the central criminal files at once.'

'I'll ring him at home,' said Bernal. 'It's high time he came up with something in this case.'

Peláez later listened to Bernal's view of the psychopath's activities.

'Yes,' he agreed, 'it holds water, but have you asked yourself why he wants to create this recurring image?'

'That's what escapes me,' said Bernal. 'If he had interfered with the victims sexually, even as a necrophiliac, it would be explicable. But apart from the trans-sexual, there's no sign of that. The earlier idea we had of a drug-ring, with the victims being addicts who were bumped off because they couldn't pay the pusher, or threatened to denounce him, is clearly wrong. It's too ordinary, too normal, to explain such abnormal behaviour. Nor do I think the idea of causing public panic during the election campaign is adequate as an explanation. The killer may have been in touch with the press, he may be gloating over the publicity, but I feel that all that is just a side-line, a bonus. It isn't the prime cause of the behaviour.'

'Have you considered the frequency of the crimes?' asked Peláez. 'They show a tendency to increase and become wilder. That is typical of one kind of criminal psychopath. What triggered this behaviour? Possibly, some similar event in his earlier life.'

'That's given me an idea,' said Bernal. 'He has this obsession with the underground railway. Would it be worth investigating incidents of a similar nature in the Metro in the past?'

'I suppose it would be,' answered Peláez, 'but remember it could have happened in any underground railway, not just the Madrid Metro. Still, it's worth a try.'

RETIRO

That evening, as the rain lashed Eugenia's pots on the terrace, Bernal was poring over large piles of reports which the Head of Metro Security had sent over by van. They covered all incidents and accidents which had occurred on the Madrid Underground since its inauguration in 1919. Bernal decided to start with the current year and work backwards, since he assumed that a man in his forties, as they had reason to believe the killer was, wouldn't have been around in 1919 to have witnessed an accident of any nature.

SOL

On Monday, 13 June, Bernal bought *Diario 16* at his local kiosk and read it over his second breakfast in Félix Pérez's.

TEN BOMBS AGAINST THE ELECTORAL PEACE!
screamed the headline, and inside there was an account
of the explosions that had occurred in the early hours
of the morning in the Basque Country, Barcelona,
Valencia, Las Palmas and the capital. Obviously a last-
ditch attempt to stop the democratic process by one
political extreme or the other, he thought. He wondered
what it would be like to vote in a free election. He'd been
too young in 1936 at the age of seventeen to have a vote,
and he supposed that for the vast majority of voters in
these elections this would be a first-time experience. He
guessed the turn-out would be high, if only because it was
an ingrained habit from the time of Franco's referenda,
when the officials checked up on the non-voters. Perhaps
Suárez would get a shock, and the country would vote
socialist. Certainly a tremendous *démarche* was in
progress within his own department, which came under
the Ministry of the Interior, to give the outward
impression of a movement towards democratization.

As he emerged from the bar on to the Calle de Alcalá,
a taxi was setting down a fare, so he took it for the short
journey to the office, to avoid the crush on the Metro. As
a result he failed to witness the latest outrage of the Metro
murderer.

SOL

After assembling his group and calling in Prieto and
Varga, Bernal went over the results of the weekend
investigations.

'Have you found any prints, Prieto?'

'I examined the clothes of the trans-sexual, especially
the skirt, which is made of quite a smooth leather
receptive to latent impressions, and I found a number of

blurred prints, and two clear ones, but these correspond to the victim himself. Of course, a number of people lifted and carried him after death, and they left their dabs as well, which I had to eliminate.' He turned to a different file. 'With regard to the wrapping paper from the dismembered pieces of human remains, I've had to get the prints of the Metro employees and policemen who picked them up and unwrapped the packages. I haven't found any clear impressions I can't otherwise account for. I think we must assume that the killer wore gloves at all times when he was handling the possibly incriminating material. I might perhaps add that it's taken us thirty hours flat out to examine all the evidence.'

'We're very grateful, Prieto,' said Bernal, 'and sorry you've had no luck with it. What about the technical analysis, Varga?'

'There is no sign on the trans-sexual's clothes of the fungoid mould we found on the clothes of the other victims and the dummies. Otherwise, chief, we've found the usual kinds of household dust and street dust. There are two points of interest: in the instep of the high-heeled shoes there is some cement powder of a formula similar to that found on the first two victims' outer clothing, but it's common enough and doesn't clinch anything by itself. What does point to the conclusion that the trans-sexual was at some point in the same place as the other victims are the pollen traces on the jacket. This morning I got a report from the Botanical Institute. They've identified the pollen as coming from a plant called a schizanthus.' Varga consulted his notes. 'It's a plant of the Solanaceae family, with finely divided leaves and showy flowers in pastel shades. They say they're often grown in pots to decorate houses and conservatories. They've sent colour photographs.'

'Pin them up on the wall, will you?' asked Bernal. 'It would be as well if everyone had a look at them in case they are spotted during our enquiries, though it's a very long shot. Anything else, Varga?'

'Nothing much, chief. The wrapping-paper and string found on the packages could have been bought in any store. The knots are of the usual sort.'

Elena Fernández and Juan Lista reported that they had visited all the old-clothes dealers they could find in the city, and none remembered having sold clothes corresponding to the description of those found on the dummies or the first two victims, nor had any of them recognized either of the Photofit pictures.

'The curious thing is,' commented Varga, 'that the clothes appear to be very old, pre-war even, in style. Not the sort of thing anyone would buy today, even second-hand.'

Bernal told them that he'd spent the previous evening working through the Metro records of accidents and injuries, to see if there was any psychological tie-up with the killer. 'I've only got back to 1964 so far, but I've picked out two incidents of possible interest. One concerns a woman who threw herself under a train in Goya station in 1973, and the other involves a series of slashings, mainly of the clothing, of women passengers in 1967. I've winkled out these reports so that we can check out the people involved in the incidents. It's amazing how many incidents occur on the Underground, but most of them are minor, involving items of lost or stolen property.'

'Has the DNI managed to identify the fingerprints of the trans-sexual, chief?' asked Ángel.

'Not yet,' said Bernal, 'but you'll realize they've only had a couple of days, and there are millions of prints in the national file. Did you get any information in the clubs last night?'

'One witness definitely recognized the photo of his friend "Carol". He claims he doesn't know his real name.

I've arranged to collect him this morning and take him down to Santa Isabel for him to view the corpse. But even so, he doesn't know where Carol lived. He thinks it was an apartment somewhere off San Bernardo, but he never visited it. He says that Carol talked of having been given a white kitten for Christmas.'

'H'm,' said Bernal, 'San Bernardo is a huge area, full of students' lodgings. It would take a lot of men to do a door-to-door enquiry. We'd perhaps do better to concentrate on the dentists, now we've made a start on them. We might make quicker progress that way. Have you sent the trans-sexual's prints to the Anti-Drugs Group, Paco?'

'Yes, chief, and they've got nothing on file.'

'This is proving to be an appallingly difficult case, as you will all be aware,' Bernal went on. 'What makes it so is the apparently random way the murderer is choosing his victims and the lack of motive. I suggest you go off now to check the dentists remaining on your lists, and show them the cast of the *travestí's* dentition. Remember they may have done a recent filling, and he may have had trouble with impacted wisdom teeth.'

RETIRO

It was only when the eastbound train on Line 2 left Banco station, where most of the travellers had got off, that the two boys noticed the large package leaning against the closed doors on the far side of the carriage.

'Hey, someone's left that behind,' whispered Miguelin to Joselito. 'There's only those two women at the other end. Let's see what it is.'

Looking sidelong at the two ladies who were chatting away, they stood up slowly and made their way to the door.

'It feels like a ham,' muttered Joselito. 'there's a plastic cover under the wrapping-paper. It's very heavy.'

'We could pinch it, and take it to my uncle's shop in Ventas,' whispered Miguelín.

'What about the cops on the platforms? They'd spot us.'

'Ha, you're chicken,' Miguelín jeered. 'I dare you.'

'Oh, OK,' said Joselito crossly. 'But we'll have to carry it between us. I can't lift it on my own.'

VENTAS

When the train pulled into the terminus station, the two boys emerged struggling under the weight of the package, and made for the exit.

'What have you got there?' asked the grey-uniformed policeman suspiciously.

'It's a ham we're delivering, señor,' said Miguelín confidently. 'It's for my uncle's shop.'

'It looks too heavy for you lads. Why didn't he have it sent by van?'

'He wanted it urgently, and offered us twenty *duros* each if we'd go and fetch it for him on the Metro.'

'He's got more money than sense, then. Be off with you, and don't drop it.'

'We won't. *Adiós, señor,*' they chorused. And they put a brave show on their ability to carry it until they got to the foot of the stairs, out of sight of the policeman.

'Phew, that was a close shave,' gasped Miguelín. 'He didn't ask our names, anyway.'

'You're crazy,' complained Joselito. 'He could have run us both in.'

BATÁN

At the Plaza de España station, terminus of the Suburbano line, Amparo Espina settled into the corner seat in the empty coach and waited for the train to move off. She clutched a bunch of marigolds and a box of chocolates, which she was taking to her sister at Aluche. She felt she was at least performing one of the corporal works of mercy, since her sister had just had a hysterectomy, but she feared her brother-in-law, and fervently hoped he would be out selling his second-hand cars. How their Mamá had tried to prevent her sister's unfortunate courtship and marriage with a man so unsuitable in every respect! The effort had killed poor Mamá, Amparo was convinced, because no one had listened, least of all her sister, whose one aim seemed to have been to get out of the family home at all costs with whatever man came along. Such a scandal! He hadn't been out of Carabanchel gaol a fortnight before her sister had married him. No wonder she'd chosen to live at Aluche, Amparo thought bitterly, it was just down the road from the prison, for when he was in the next time.

When the doors closed and the train moved off, Amparo noticed the box on the seat which was diagonally opposite her. That's strange, she thought, she hadn't seen anyone come in. She looked along the coach. Ah well, someone had left it behind on the previous journey.

After its descent into the tunnel that ran under the river Manzanares, the train chugged up the incline and emerged into the open air before reaching El Lago station. Amparo gazed out at the remnants of the Civil War trenches between the trees in the Casa de Campo without seeing them. Her mind dwelt on her sister's wickedness and what it had done to their saintly Mamá. She was glad she had not been so foolish as to marry. Now, at 52, she had the family home guaranteed to her by law for the rest of her days, so long as she didn't get wed, and her brother-in-law could rant and rave about his wife's share of the patrimony as much as he liked; but the law was the law. Amparo had spent 10,000 pesetas on solicitors' fees to prove it. Well worth it, every penny, to discover she had absolute security.

At El Lago, four scruffily uniformed soldiers got in, looked at Amparo and grimaced. She noticed the reaction and was well pleased. Safe, safe at last from lascivious glances, that was the gift that age had bestowed on her. To the right of the train the ferris-wheel and roller-coaster at the Parque de Atracciones could be seen. Amparo remembered one visit to the place with horror. Mamá, widowed a year, had taken her two daughters there, considering that they needed a change of scene from the house of gloom, with its black-draped photographs of their father, now in glory. Amparo had been persuaded by her sister to get on an undulating roundabout, and her long hair had got caught in the mechanical sunshade, which was made of yellow ribbed silk to resemble the back of a caterpillar. She only remembered how long she had screamed before the machine came to a rest and the attendants had freed her.

The train had picked up speed before reaching the long curve that led into Batán station, which was the alighting point for the fun-fair. When the train lurched violently, the box on the seat opposite Amparo fell over and its lid flew off. When the severed head with the long blonde hair rolled across the carriage floor to her feet, Amparo's screams echoed down the years, and brought the soldiers running to her side.

ATOCHA

At four o'clock that afternoon, Bernal was back in Peláez's dissecting room viewing the almost complete remains of what had probably been the Metro murderer's first victim.

'The grocer had a nasty shock, Peláez, when his nephew brought the torso in, thinking it was a ham.'

'I can imagine,' said Peláez. 'But what with the price of ham and other *fiambres* they probably thought at first they were on to a good thing, finding it in the Metro like that. What action are you taking against them?'

'Just a stern warning to the boys. They were only ten and had a severe shock as it was. The grocer did ring the police at once when he realized the remains were human.'

'And the head?' asked Peláez. 'That was found on the Suburbano, wasn't it?'

'Yes, and the unfortunate maiden lady at whose feet it landed is now in the psychiatric ward under heavy sedation. Oddly, she kept on gabbling about a caterpillar. The doctors couldn't make head or tail of it. The Civil Guard lieutenant who dealt with her at Batán said she seemed to have flipped completely. The incident aroused some childhood memory for her in that very place, apparently.'

'Well,' said Peláez, gazing critically at his handiwork on the slab, 'we've got nearly all of this cadaver now. Only the left hand and the right foot missing. I'm sure all these parts fit together. There's only one body, and no bits of any other.'

'That's a relief,' said Bernal. 'The press haven't rung you, have they?'

'Not yet,' answered Peláez, 'but I've given instructions that no information is to be given.'

'They've got wind of it', said Bernal, 'from Saturday's

discoveries, but they don't know about today's, so far as we know.'

'You can't blame them, Bernal, it's quite a story. Have you seen the hæmatologist's report? He's sent me a copy.'

'Yes, and as I interpret it, reading among the jargon, the blood found in the mouths of the dummies and the three whole cadavers came from this dismembered corpse.'

'That's his conclusion,' said Peláez. 'The killer must have bled this first one like a stuck pig and preserved the blood by mixing it with the trichloroethylene for later use. My task now is to find the cause of death in this dismembered victim. It's one hell of a problem because of the putrefaction, and the dissection, which was artistically done. By one of the profession, it seems.' Peláez pondered over the corpse. 'Try to get inside his mind, then you'll catch him.'

'I've been trying to do just that. Do you mind if I go off now? I'm feeling a bit queasy. It's the smell of the formalin; it always turns my stomach.'

'The whole business upsets you. I wonder you didn't choose another profession.'

'Too late to change now.'

SOL

By 7.45 p.m. on the same day, the detectives belonging to Bernal's group one by one trotted wearily up the stairs to the office.

'None of you had any luck with the dentists?' asked Bernal. 'How many more are there to see?'

'We're about half way through the main list,' said Navarro, 'but there are more in the outer suburbs.'

'What about the ones in the San Bernardo district where "Carol"'s friend thought he had a flat?'

'We've done them all without result.'

'It amazes me how they can tell anyway,' said Elena. 'The photo of the face is not good, and one mouth looks much like another to me.'

'Remember how long they peer into each one,' said Bernal. 'The risk is they won't remember the face that goes with it; but they can often turn up the record in their files on the basis of the mouth picture alone.' He went on to tell them about the discovery of the head and torso and of Peláez's fitting together of the pieces. 'The corpse is female, aged 22 to 24, with blonde hair and blue eyes. Much putrefaction has taken place, apparently in a cool, damp place, with the result that adipocere is beginning to form, which suggests that this death took place some six to eight weeks ago. I'm sorry to tell you that we have an extra cast of a dentition to track down tomorrow to try to identify this girl as well as the trans-sexual. Peláez has noticed a recent extraction of the second left lower molar in the girl's case, so you will be able to ask about that.'

There was a general groan as they realized they might have to revisit all the dentists they had already interviewed.

'You'd better all get some rest,' added Bernal. 'Tomorrow is the day of contemplation before Wednesday's general election. So you should find the dentists working, but Election Day will be a different matter.'

When they had left, Bernal received a telephone call.

'It's me, Luchi. What happened to you this afternoon?'

'I tried to ring you at the bank before you left, Consuelo, but I missed you. The Metro murderer is cutting up the victims now.'

'Oh God, how ghastly. Don't forget you're taking me to Portazgo in half an hour, to the socialist *mitin*.'

'Oh Lord, I'd forgotten all about it. Do I have to?'

'You promised, Luchi. I'll meet you at the corner of Carretas in ten minutes.'

PORTAZGO

Line 1 was packed as Bernal and Consuelo Lozano fought for room to breathe. Most of their fellow travellers were fellow-travellers indeed, wearing plastic lapel-stickers depicting a hand holding a red rose, the symbol of the PSOE — the Spanish Workers' Socialist Party. Luis felt uncomfortable in his blue office suit, but Consuelo was resplendent in a red frock with a red chiffon scarf tied round her neck, and her eyes shone with political fervour.

'Isn't it exciting, Luchi? All these people expressing their true feelings for the first time for thirty-eight years?' She exuded an expensive Parisian perfume, perhaps Givenchy, as she began to perspire in the crush, and it excited him.

He grunted a noncommittal reply as the train drew into Portazgo station and hundreds streamed off it to join the many thousands already crammed into the Rayo Vallecano football stadium.

The street outside was a seething mass, with vendors offering red and gold favours and posters, and cassettes of the *Internationale*, the *Himno de Riego* — the nineteenth-century revolutionary anthem — and *Els Segadors*, the Catalonian left-wing song. Consuelo led him through the turnstiles and battled her way to the upper tier of the stadium.

'We're a bit far away, but we'll see everything from here. Why don't you climb on to that balustrade?'

'I'll get giddy and fall,' complained Luis. 'You know I've no head for heights.'

Just then a helicopter could be heard, and there was a roar from the crowd as news of Felipe González's arrival spread around the stadium. A procession of girls dressed in red were brandishing party banners and they advanced towards the podium at one end of the football pitch, while the loudspeakers began to blaze with the strains of the *Internationale*, which the crowd immediately took up.

'How do they know the words, Luchi? It's been banned for years.'

'A kind of folk memory, I suppose. The older ones teach the younger ones as they go along.'

He watched a family group alongside them with fascination. The son, daughter and son-in-law held up the children for them to see the stadium, while the grandmother, poorly dressed in black, wiped away tears — of joy, he had no doubt — but of remembrance also. In spirit the old woman seemed to have gone back forty years, to the Second Republic, and was overcome by the experience.

'*¡Felipe, capullo! ¡Queremos uno tuyo!* — Felipe, rosebud! We want one of yours!' chanted the crowd enthusiastically, in that eerie double-stressed rhythm. And they went on to chant the most scurrilous slogans about the right-wing politicians: '*¡******, *cabrón! ¡Bájate el pantalón!* — *****, you bastard! Get your trousers down!'

Personalization, that was what was wrong with politics, decided Bernal: they created heroes, who soon disappointed them, just as they did with footballers and pop-singers. They couldn't, or didn't want to look behind the face for the idea, most of the time. He had to admit that the speech, what he could hear of it through the booming loudspeakers and the frequent and fervent interruptions, was intelligent and skilful. An orator with charisma, he thought, we've got one again. The slight Andalusian accent gave the utterance a slightly simple air, which made it sound more sincere. As the mass euphoria reached its peak, he suddenly began to sympathize with his wife's views: it was going to happen all over again.

'Let's go, Consuelo, before the crowd blocks the exits.'

ALONSO MARTÍNEZ

On Tuesday, 14 June, the Day of National Contemplation, the dactyloscopic experts working in the fingerprint files of the Documento Nacional de Identidad identified the thumb and right index-finger prints of the dead trans-sexual 'Carol'. The photograph on the record card bore little resemblance to Eusebio Flores García in the female guise he had assumed when found at Concepción underground station, but the card revealed an address in La Carihuela (Málaga) for the year 1976, which was sufficient for Bernal to enlist the aid of the Málaga police.

SOL

By midday Bernal had an address for Flores in Madrid, which the local inspector at Benalmádena had obtained from the dead man's sister. She was also on her way on the late morning TALGO express to identify the corpse.

Bernal and Varga set out in the official car for the Calle del Norte, after requesting the Inspector in charge of Universidad District to meet them at the address. Bernal left word with Navarro for his detectives, when they returned at lunch-time, to concentrate now on identifying only the dentition of the dismembered corpse.

NOVICIADO

Inspector Gravina of Universidad Comisaría was waiting for Bernal and Varga in the doorway of the house in the Calle del Norte, which was a narrow street parallel to San

Bernardo, behind the records office of the Ministry of Justice.

'*¿Qué tal, Gravina?* — How are things?' Bernal greeted him with warmth. 'It's been a long time since we worked together.'

Gravina flushed with pleasure and remarked on how they had cooperated on the San Bernardo chocolate-shop case more than twenty years earlier.

'Have you talked to the porter, Gravina?'

'Not yet, Superintendent. I thought I'd leave it all to you, since it's connected with the Metro murders. He's sitting in his office. I've left the uniformed men in my car in case they're needed, but I didn't want to arouse idle curiosity in the neighbourhood.'

'Well done. We'll have a chat with the porter first.'

They entered the old house, where a wide wooden staircase rose into the gloomy stairwell.

'*Buenos días.* We're from the Dirección General de Seguridad,' Bernal said politely to the porter, showing him his metal *placa* bearing the imperial eagle. 'Have you a tenant called Flores?'

The porter scratched his head in puzzlement. 'Oh, you mean Carol, the *travestí*? Yes, she's got the attic apartment. It's a long climb up there, I can tell you. Haven't seen her for a couple of days. She must have gone to her sister's in Málaga.'

'Have you got a key to her apartment?'

'No, sir, I haven't. The owner of the flats will have one, but he lives in El Pozuelo.'

'Have you got his telephone number?' asked Bernal.

'Yes, it's on this list.'

'Well, ring him and see if he's at home. Then let me speak to him.'

The porter dialled the number, but the phone went on ringing without being answered. 'He's not in by the looks of it.'

'Varga, have you brought your tools so that we can effect an entry?'

'Yes, chief.'

'Gravina, perhaps you would ring the duty judge to warn him, and ask him if he wishes to exercise his right to be present.'

While Gravina was phoning the Juzgado de Guardia, Bernal questioned the porter further. 'How long has this Carol lived here?'

'More than a year. He's a quiet tenant. Doesn't hold wild parties or anything like that. Has something happened to him?'

'We're not sure yet. Do many friends call to see him?'

'One or two, but they looked to be *travestís* like he is. He's quite harmless really, but some of the other tenants have complained.'

'Do you know where he works?' asked Bernal.

'He's had a number of jobs and never seems to keep any of them long, once they find out he isn't really a girl. Mind, I think they must be daft to think so in the first place, because his voice gives him away, but the employers don't seem to notice until they receive his social security documents.'

'Where is he employed now?'

'In a flower-shop on the Gran Vía, I think. At least he told me a fortnight ago he was starting there. Before that he'd been a manicurist in a hairdresser's salon.'

'Did he get a lot of mail?' asked Bernal.

The porter pointed to the green mailboxes on the wall of the hallway. 'It's the end box there. I've never seen much in it. Circulars mainly.'

Gravina came back from the telephone. 'The magistrate says he will leave it to you, Superintendent, but he naturally wants you to call him if you find any human remains. He'd like a report in due course.'

'That's all right, then. Varga will pick the lock.'

After they had climbed up the six flights of stairs, Bernal and Gravina waited while Varga inspected the lock, which he managed to open in two or three minutes, using a *ganzúa* or skeleton-key. As he opened the outer door, which led into a small hallway, they could hear faint mewing sounds.

'That'll be the white kitten one of his friends talked about,' said Bernal. 'Watch he doesn't make a run for the landing.'

Being careful not to touch anything, Varga switched on the light in the hallway using a pair of pliers, and slowly opened the inner door.

They were surprised to see a room filled with sunlight, which streamed in from large windows overlooking the rooftops of the houses that stretched down to the Plaza de España. Their nostrils were assailed by the cloying smell of decaying flowers.

On a large bed, covered with a pink silk bedspread, there lay a small Persian kitten, which raised its head weakly when it saw them.

'It'll be starving,' said Bernal. 'You could take it down to the porter, Varga, and see if he's got some milk. Then you should phone Prieto to come and fingerprint everything, just in case the killer came to this apartment.'

As they waited, Bernal and Gravina gazed at the room in astonishment. It had a quite extraordinary décor of pink drapes, and it was dominated by a three-foot high statue of the Virgin, dressed in ornate robes and crowned by a gilt halo. She was holding a minuscule infant Christ in her arms. The image was flanked by two very large Talavera vases, each filled with dying pink and white gladioli arranged in a fan-shape.

'Have you ever seen anything like it, Superintendent?' Gravina whispered almost in awe.

'It looks like a cross between a Parisian brothel and a Lady chapel,' commented Bernal more loudly. 'I think

that statue is a copy in reduced size of Nuestra Señora de
la Victoria, which is in a church in Málaga. Flores, being
from Carihuela, would adopt her as his patron saint, of
course.'

Varga now returned and reported that Prieto and his
assistant were on their way.

'Open that fitted wardrobe for us, Varga, and let's see
what's inside,' Bernal requested.

'You've never seen so much stuff, chief!' exclaimed
Varga. 'These two cupboards hold ladies' clothes, and
there are some men's garments in the corner one. And
fifteen pairs of high-heeled shoes!'

Bernal turned to a dressing-table fitted with three
mirrors, which was adorned with a pleated pink silk
valance. 'He used an enormous number of cosmetics,
didn't he? It'll take Prieto a long time to fingerprint all
these pots and jars. I think it'll be better for me to return
this afternoon, after Prieto's finished. I especially want to
see any papers and correspondence you come across.'

SOL

When the post arrived at midday, Navarro noticed that it
contained a small parcel wrapped in brown paper
addressed in curiously printed Gothic capitals to 'Supt.
Bernal, Brigada Criminal, Gobernación, Puerta del Sol'.

On Bernal's return from the Calle del Norte, Paco
drew his attention to the parcel. 'There's no sender's
name on it, and the post-mark is blurred, chief.'

'You'd better take it to Varga's lab, Paco. Handle it as
little as possible. I've got a hunch it contains something
very unpleasant.'

Varga's chief assistant began to test the package with
various types of equipment. 'There's nothing metallic in
it, Inspector.'

'Could there be explosives?'

'I'll X-ray it first, then we'll open it by remote control. I'll be able to demonstrate our latest toy for you.'

Navarro followed him to a scanner, into which he placed the parcel. 'You'd better take a look yourself, Inspector.'

Paco found himself examining an eerie, greenish picture of the bones of a human hand and foot. 'It's the rest of the dismembered corpse,' he said gravely. 'The killer's getting cheeky. You can open it up now, but don't smudge any latent prints there may be on the wrappings. What do you make of the printed address?'

'It's been done with a home printing-set. You can buy them in any stationer's, but the letters will have unique irregularities, just like the letters of a typewriter, so we'll be able to identify the printing-set if you find it. I'll still open it with our new toy, in case it's booby-trapped, though it seems unlikely, since there are no wires.'

The assistant took Navarro to a specially constructed room, with blast walls a metre thick, in which there was a small inspection-window of toughened glass and levers which operated mechanical arms inside the chamber. 'I'll show you how we can open it by remote control. These arms can do almost anything you or I could do by touching the package itself.'

After some minutes of manœuvring, the parcel was opened and was revealed to contain only a shoe-box and the missing limbs of the Metro murderer's first victim. After Bernal had been called to the laboratory and had ascertained that the newly discovered left hand also had the skin removed from the fingertips, he left instructions for the remains to be taken to Dr Peláez, and the box and wrapping-paper to be checked for prints.

Back in his office he discussed the matter with Navarro. 'Why should he change the pattern of leaving the dismembered remains in the Metro and send these last two pieces to me?'

'A gesture of defiance, chief?' suggested Paco. 'A sort of challenge?'

'Yes, that's possible. He must have seen the television news item yesterday evening, and the evening papers. Check the post-mark with Correos and see if they can find out the posting office and the time of posting. It's possible some employee may recognize one of the Photofit pictures.'

NOVICIADO

Early that evening, Varga and Bernal went over the trans-sexual's apartment with especial care.

'There aren't many letters, *jefe*,' said Varga. 'Most of them are from his sister in Málaga, who seems to have sent him money from time to time. The others are receipts for various bills.'

'Any accounts from his dentist among them, Varga?'

'No, chief. But look, here's a small appointment book in the dressing-table drawer.'

'Let me see the last entries in it,' said Bernal. 'H'm, "*11 June, 9 a.m., dentist*". Pity he didn't put down the dentist's name. He may have been one of the last people to see Flores alive. Have you found an address book?'

'No, chief.'

'Well, there are a few addresses noted down in the back of this appointment diary.' Bernal flicked over the mainly blank pages. 'He didn't have much of a social life, or at least, he didn't bother to note the engagements down. Some of the entries seem to refer to interviews for jobs, to judge by the firms listed.' Bernal put the book down. 'These clothes will take some days to examine. We'll get Elena to help you with the women's stuff. You'd best pack

it all up and take it back to the lab. I think we've done all
we can here for the moment.'

SOL

At 7.30 p.m. the same evening, Bernal looked out of the
window into the Calle de Carretas, where convoys of cars,
with the horns blowing rhythmically, were tearing across
Sol and up towards the Plaza de Benavente. Youths were
clinging to their roofs and bonnets waving the red and
gold national flag.

'I think they're Falangists,' said Navarro, 'doing some
last-minute canvassing.'

Bernal noticed some well-dressed ladies on the corner
of Sol giving the extended-arm salute as the cars passed.
'*¡Viva Franco! ¡Arriba España!*' they shrilled. '*¡Arriba!*' the
youths shouted back. '*¡Los rojos al paredón!*—The Reds
to the firing-squad!'

'I hope they won't meet the socialists and communists
at Atocha,' said Navarro, 'or our colleagues in Anti-
disturbios will have quite a night of it.'

'I think we'd better go home, Paco. I've got to read a
lot more of those old reports on incidents in the Metro.
No one has phoned in with an identification by a dentist
of the dentition of the dismembered girl, have they?'

'No, chief, nothing at all.'

'I'm fearful about this case, Paco. The killer is clever
and cool. People around him probably haven't noticed
anything strange in his manner. But he must have got a
workshop or cellar which doesn't arouse suspicion, where
he made the dummies and cut up the first victim.'

RETIRO

By eleven o'clock that night, after picking at a chickpea stew filled with slices of blood-sausage—another of Eugenia's country recipes—Bernal had read the Metropolitan Company's reports back to 1940, and from these he had pulled out three for further enquiry. He found them fascinating reading as he got back to the Civil War period. There had been fewer lines in those days, and clearly the numbers of passengers carried were far lower than in the modern period. Out of curiosity, he looked up the annual *Memorias* the Company Director had provided. Yes, in 1968, 448 million passengers had been carried, compared with 181 millions in 1940. Then there had existed only twenty-one km. of track, compared with more than fifty km. today. The Metro had even carried soldiers part of the way to the front to defend Madrid against Franco's insurgents.

After a further half-hour spent reading the reports, Bernal's eye was caught by the account of an accident that had taken place on 16 March 1939: a girl called Lidia Cortés Díaz, aged 12, had died by being crushed against a soldier's bayonet on Sol platform during the evening rush hour. Bernal had a vivid memory of how carelessly arms had been carried during the Civil War. The girl's tiny brother who was with her had lost control of his nerves and had threatened vengeance for her death. What struck Bernal so forcibly was the faded police photograph attached to the report: it showed Lidia's corpse stretched out on the platform, her blonde hair awry and blood trickling from the corner of her mouth. This reminded him strongly of the way the dummies and the three murder victims had been found. The dead sister even bore some likeness to the first two Metro victims. Was this the killer's recurrent image which he imposed on the scene?

Bernal wondered where Lidia's brother was now. If he had been some years younger than she, say between five and eight, that would make him between forty-three and forty-six — about the right age for the suspect spotted at Cuatro Caminos station. Was it feasible that someone could nurse a grievance, however intensely felt, against the Metropolitan Company, or society at large, for nearly forty years to a point where he was spurred into committing such terrible crimes? He would have to discuss it with Peláez, and possibly with one of the city's leading psychiatrists. And the first urgent task would be to trace Lidia's brother.

GENERAL MOLA

On Election day, 15 June, Bernal went to vote early before going to the office. At the polling-station he found the president of the table in despair, because *militantes* of the extreme right had come in when the doors opened and had removed all the parties' ballot-papers except their own, which meant a long delay while spares were sent for from the Escuela Aguirre nearby. Fortunately Bernal had brought with him the ballot-paper sent by post to each household. While he was there, the *guardia* was called from the entrance to another of the electoral tables, where an old man, outraged at finding that his name had been omitted from the census list, had raised his walking-stick and smashed the glass electoral urn in which some early voters had already cast their voting-papers, thereby invalidating all those votes. He was arrested and taken to the Comisaría. Otherwise everything seemed to be going off peaceably, in the Salamanca quarter at least.

SOL

At the office Bernal put Navarro on to the task of
tracking down Lidia Cortés Díaz's younger brother, whose
christian name didn't appear in the Metropolitan
Company's report for 16 March 1939. But the dead girl's
address was given, and with that information and the
DNI files running continuously from April 1939, as well
as the old records surviving from the Second Republic, he
might be traced in a few days.

At 9 a.m. they received a call from Juan Lista.
'Superintendent? I think I'm on to something. At least,
I've got a feeling about it.'

Bernal always trusted Lista's 'feelings' which had
proved to be right so often in the past. 'What is it, Lista?'

'Well, chief, I was getting towards the end of my list of
dentists yesterday evening, in the Avenida de Concha
Espina, just above the Plaza de los Sagrados Corazones.
The address turned out to be one of those older houses on
the hill. A young receptionist told me to wait and she took
the photo of the dental cast into the dentist. But she soon
returned and said he'd gone off, having seen his last
patient for the day. She asked if I'd come back today. I
gained the definite impression that she was lying, or that
she was frightened. I've just gone back there, and the
surgery door is shut, with a "closed" notice up.'

'Well, what makes you think anything is wrong except
for the receptionist's manner yesterday evening?' asked
Bernal. 'After all, it's Election Day, and she probably
forgot about that.'

'It's not just that, chief. It's the plants behind a glass
partition alongside the private entrance at the side of the
house. They look like the ones on the photos sent over by
the Botanical Institute.'

'I'll bring Varga over with me. Give me the exact
address. Perhaps you'd wait outside the house for us,' said

Bernal. 'What's the dentist's name, by the way?'

'Roberto Cortés Díaz.'

'He could be our man, Lista. If he comes out, hold him on any pretext until we get there. If he tries to get away, use your service pistol.'

In the end Bernal took Varga the technician and two plainclothesmen, and they sped along the Calle de Alcalá and up the Castellana with siren screaming and blue light flashing. When they turned into the lower end of Concha Espina, Bernal ordered the driver to turn off the siren and warning light. 'We don't want to give him too much notice.'

ALFONSO XIII

In front of the house they found Lista waiting. 'No one's gone in or come out, chief. As you can see, the surgery door faces the street, while the private entrance is at the side, where there's a garage at basement level. I spotted the schizanthus plants through the glass panel alongside the private door.'

'And no one answered your knock, Lista?'

'No, chief, so I went down the road to the telephone kiosk to call you. Can I ask why you think Cortés may be the killer?'

'I found something in the Metro records for 1939, believe it or not. We'll knock again, and ring the surgery bell. Paco has rung the District Inspector to tell him we were on our way. He should turn up shortly.' Despite their knocking and ringing, no one answered either door. 'Varga, you'll have to open the house door for us. I'll carry the can if we're making a terrible mistake. You two men', Bernal addressed the plainclothesmen, 'had better wait one at each door in case he makes a run for it.'

Varga got the door open in a very short time, and with pistols drawn they entered the glass-panelled hallway, adorned with pots of schizanthus. Varga opened the inner door and listened. All that could be heard was a light tapping sound coming from a room along the corridor and the ticking of a large wall-clock. They advanced along the corridor, looking into each room in turn, until they reached the closed door from behind which came the tapping noise. Lista turned the handle and opened the door very slightly, with great caution, while Bernal stood to one side with his pistol at the ready. Lista peeped through the widening crack and gestured to Bernal, and they burst into the room.

They were surprised to see only the diminutive figure of an old lady seated in a rocking-chair in which she gently moved to and fro, her gnarled hands grasping the carved wooden arms tightly. Bernal made a sign to Lista and Varga to search the kitchen quarters at the back of the house, and he came up to the old lady, who turned her head sightlessly towards the partly drawn window-blinds.

'I'm sorry to disturb you, señora. I'm looking for Señor Cortés.'

She gave no indication that she had heard or seen him, and Bernal realized from the drooped appearance of the facial muscles and the mouth that she had suffered some sort of stroke or paralysis. She was very, very old, and wore a white lace cap in a style not seen since the early part of the century.

The room was crammed with nineteenth-century bric-à-brac, and on a small table covered with a gold chenille cloth at her side stood a row of family photographs in tarnished silver frames, with a small bunch of violets in a vase in front of them. Which of the photographs was of Lidia Cortés Díaz, Bernal wondered. But he did not dare approach too close.

Lista and Varga returned and indicated that the

ground floor was otherwise unoccupied.

'I don't think she's aware of our presence,' whispered Bernal. 'It's curious there's no servant looking after her. Let's search the upstairs.'

The house was old and had a large number of rooms, most of which had an air of disuse. On the first landing, a number of doors faced them, but inside the bedrooms and bathroom they found no one, and nothing seemed disturbed. From the landing a long gallery, in which there hung a series of nineteenth-century portraits in oils, perhaps of earlier heads of the family, led to another wing of the house. When they reached the imposing door at the end, they found it locked.

'Can you get this open, Varga, without our having to break it down?' Bernal said quietly to the technician.

'I'll have a go, *jefe*,' whispered Varga, producing a bunch of peculiar-looking keys.

After a few moments, he succeeded in picking the lock and Bernal motioned to the others to take cover as he opened the door, at the same time drawing his service pistol. No sound came from the darkened room. He felt for the light switch and was suddenly dazzled by the brightness as some big spotlights came on. He pushed the door open little by little, and peered in. There was no one there.

'Come on in,' he said, 'It's deserted.'

They were all astonished by the scene. At the end of the room, the spotlights picked out a national flag and two gold-framed portraits: one was of José Antonio Primo de Rivera, founder of Falange Española, the fascist party of the 'thirties, and the other depicted General Franco in the uniform of a captain-general, wearing the red sash of the Laureate Cross of St Ferdinand. The room, they realized, was really a museum of Spanish Fascism, with framed photographs and posters covering all its walls, under which stood showcases containing weapons of the period.

'Phew!' exclaimed Varga. 'It's just like the Army Museum.'

'Quite a collection,' said Bernal drily. 'This gives us some insight into the killer's obsessions.'

They found nothing of interest in the rest of the upper floors, and descended again to the entrance hall. Here Lista pointed to a small door they hadn't noticed earlier. It was locked, but Varga picked the lock in a few moments. They now found themselves in the professional part of the residence, in a hallway done out in the latest style which contained the receptionist's desk and doors labelled 'waiting-room', 'surgery' and 'dental laboratory'.

Bernal opened the door leading to the street and spoke to the second plainclothesman stationed outside. 'Has the local inspector arrived yet?'

'Not yet, sir.'

This part of the building also proved to be deserted. Bernal and Varga examined the laboratory with particular interest, but they found it contained only dental casts and plates in various stages of preparation.

'Have a look at the filing-cabinets, Lista, and see if you can find out the name and address of the receptionist; then we'll get her brought in. The bird's clearly flown. I'll ring through and put out an all-units call on Cortés Díaz. The DNI should be able to produce the photograph on his most recent *carnet de identidad*. I'll get Paco to put a check on all outgoing flights from Barajas and a watch for him at the railway termini. He must have had a vehicle of some sort, Lista. Try to find out its registration number, then we'll pass it on to Paco. Cortés must have been tipped off by your questioning of his receptionist yesterday evening and guessed we'd be on to him today.'

Lista returned from the filing-cabinets triumphant from a hasty search of their contents. He showed Bernal a filing card. 'It's all very orderly. Here's the receptionist's name and address and her social security papers. She lives out at the Plaza de Castilla, but she's on the phone.'

'Ring her and see if she'll come in. Don't tell her what it's about.'

Bernal went over the geography of the dental surgery again, looking for the storeroom or basement they had supposed the killer must have had, but he could find none. He could see the surgery had the very latest equipment: an automated patient's chair and high-speed drill unit, and an X-ray machine in the corner of the room. He and Varga searched the laboratory again, but there were no hidden doors, or trapdoors in the floor. Yet the house looked old enough to have cellars.

Bernal rang Navarro: 'Send Ángel and Carlos as soon as they report in. And send Elena; we've got an old lady who's been left alone here. She'll have to be taken to a place where she can be cared for.'

To satisfy his immediate curiosity, Bernal looked into the patients' files, which were stored in alphabetical order in grey metal cabinets. He sighed with satisfaction. The case was becoming clearer in his mind.

The first plainclothesman called to him through the connecting door from the hallway of the house. 'Could you come, Superintendent? A servant-woman has arrived.'

A short woman in her late fifties, carrying a shopping-basket full of vegetables, was standing nervously in the hall.

'What is happening? Is the señora all right?' she asked in alarm.

'Yes, yes,' Bernal reassured her. 'You can attend to her in a moment. We're from the Dirección General de Seguridad. Have you seen Señor Cortés today?'

'I made breakfast for Don Roberto as usual at 8.30. I usually go out to buy fresh croissants near the Plaza on my way back from seven o'clock Mass. As I say, I put hot coffee and the buns for the señor in the dining-room, but he didn't touch any of it. I went out again then to do the shopping for lunch. Has something happened to him?'

'It's just that we want to interview him very urgently. What is your name?'

'Pilar Vila.' The servant-woman had that severe dress and downtrodden look so common in a class of domestic servants recruited in the country villages and now fast disappearing.

'Have you been with the family long?' asked Bernal in a kindly manner.

'More than forty-six years, since the señora was quite a young woman. There were five of us in the old señor's service: a cook, a scullery maid, a parlourmaid, a butler and myself. I was the señora's personal maid, but I have to do everything single-handed now,' she said rather bitterly. 'It was a big establishment then, but after the war everything changed.'

'How many children were there?' Bernal asked her.

'Fourteen, and there'd been a nanny to look after them when they were young, and they had private tutors. All but one of the surviving ones are married and never come here now, except on the señora's birthday, and at Christmas.'

'How old is the señora?'

'Eighty last birthday, and she's had three strokes which have left her quite incapacitated. I really ought to go and see to her.'

'You shall, you shall,' Bernal soothed her. 'I've only a few more questions for the moment. The rest will keep for later on. Now, the other children. One of them is Don Roberto, the dentist?'

'Yes, he's the only other one now. Poor Lidia was killed in a tragic accident in the last days of the war. Oh, she was a charming girl; she filled the house with laughter. She died a month before her thirteenth birthday.'

'And how did she come to die?'

'A stupid accident in the Metro at Sol station. She was pressed by the crowd as a train full of armed soldiers arrived, and a carelessly-held bayonet transfixed her. She bled to death. Don Roberto was with her at the time—he was only a tiny tot then. It affected him greatly; he was never the same afterwards. And the shock killed her poor father. He died a year later; I think of a broken heart. After that, nothing was the same in this house. Can I attend to Doña Laura now?'

'Yes, yes, of course. But tell me, has Don Roberto got a car?'

'Yes, a large French car, which has one of those doors at the back.'

'A shooting-brake?'

'Yes, that's it. He went out in it this morning, because it's not there now.'

'And apart from the dental laboratory, has he got another storeroom in the house?'

'Well, there's the cellar, where he does his sculpture. That's his hobby, you know. But he never lets me down there to clean it. He keeps it locked, always.'

'Where is the entrance to it?'

'There's a cupboard-door under the stairs. I'll show you, but I don't know where he keeps the keys.'

SOL

Roberto Cortés Díaz stood on the pavement at the corner of Montera and Sol, looking across at the Gobernación building. He appeared to be oblivious of the mass of people around him and of the screaming loudspeakers of the election-vans urging people to go to vote.

He had realized at once the previous evening that the caller who showed his receptionist the photograph of a dentition was a detective, probably from Bernal's group. After glancing at it, he'd told her to say he'd already left. That would gain him time, he knew. He'd been shaken at nine o'clock that morning when he was about to have his breakfast to see the same man banging on the surgery door. He knew Pilar had gone out to the market to do the shopping. He watched the man try the house door, and then walk away down the hill. Roberto took his chance and drove the car out of the garage and away up the hill.

Bernal might be starting to suspect him, but what evidence did he have against him? None. He'd show him he could outwit even a *superpolicía*. Roberto clutched the long package he was carrying more tightly as he began to cross the Puerta del Sol.

ALFONSO XIII

Inspector Quintana of Chamartín District and two uniformed men had now arrived at the house in Concha Espina, and Bernal explained to the local inspector his suspicions about the dentist, Roberto Cortés Díaz. 'Would you ring the duty judge, Quintana, and tell him we're making an unauthorized search of the premises, on grounds of extreme urgency?'

In the meantime, Lista had discovered the documents relating to Cortés's car in the drawer of an escritoire, and he was phoning them through to Navarro, for onward transmission to Traffic Control.

Varga found that the cellar door had an old-fashioned lock, as well as a modern tumble-lock which presented no difficulty. The older lock took him much longer to pick. With the door open at last, he called Superintendent Bernal, and he felt for a light switch. The steps were now dimly lit, but at the bottom there was almost complete darkness.

'I can't find the light switch down here, chief,' said Varga, switching on an electric torch, the beam of which he directed round the cellar. In its rays they were astonished to see rows of female figures, some standing, others sitting or lying, and all looking rather similar to one another. 'Here's the source of the dummies, chief. I'll see if the light switch is on the other side.'

Suddenly the basement was brightly illuminated by two neon tubes which flicked on, and they could see they were in a large workshop, with two benches on which lay cut sheets of polystyrene.

'There are more than twenty of those figures, chief,' said Varga, 'and they all look alike. What did he make them for?'

'I think they're all meant to look like his sister, as he remembered her just before her death,' said Bernal quietly. 'Where do you think he dismembered the body of the first victim?'

Varga searched the cement floor carefully. 'No sign of bloodstains here. But there's another door at the far end. I'll see what's in there.' Varga opened the narrow door which led into an inner cellar. 'There's a bathroom here, chief, and some sheets of polythene tacked to the floor.'

Bernal joined him to make a visual inspection. 'The bath's been cleaned up, Varga, but there are some small brown stains around the drain. Can you do the test for blood?'

'I'll go and fetch my bag.'

While Varga was getting his equipment, Bernal searched around for the surgical instruments which the killer would have needed. In a small cupboard he found a long black case, which he opened with extreme care, in order not to spoil any latent prints. Inside gleamed a set of surgeon's tools, including a saw.

When Varga returned, Bernal pointed to the case. 'He had the means to cut her up, and I suppose he would have studied some anatomy in the first part of his dentistry course.'

'I'll test the saw in a moment, chief.'

Varga prepared a small sheet of white blotting paper, which he pressed gently on to the brown stains in the bath. Then with a glass dropper he placed a few drops of a saturated solution of benzidine in glacial acetic acid on to the absorbent paper, which turned blue where it had touched the suspect stains.

'It's positive, chief, although, of course, fresh fruit or milk would give a similar result. I'll just try the leucomalachite test.'

With a clean knife, he scraped a little of the brown stain on to a fresh filter paper, and with a tiny glass rod he placed a drop of the reagent alongside the powdered brown substance from the bath. He set his stop-watch, and after ten seconds the stain turned green. Bernal looked on in fascination as Varga kept an eye on his watch. After a minute had passed, the stain turned greenish-blue. 'It's definitely blood, chief, but we can't tell if it's human or animal until the hæmatologist does the Teichmann and Strzyzowski microchemical tests in the lab.'

'Still,' said Bernal, 'there's plenty of circumstantial evidence to go on for the moment. You realize that Paloma Ledesma, María Luz Cabrera and Flores were all patients of his? That's the connection between the victims which has eluded us all along. See if you can find their clothes, and the source of the old clothes.'

'Some of those mannequins are dressed in old clothes,' Varga pointed out. 'I'll inspect them back in the lab for signs of that saprophytic mould. It certainly smells damp down here.'

'And where did he hide the body of the first victim before dismembering it? There are sure to be traces.'

'I'll make a thorough search, chief, but may I call for

my assistants to come? There's too much for me to cope with alone.'

'Of course,' said Bernal. 'I'm expecting Navarro to send Miranda and Gallardo over when they report in. They can search the upper floors. I'll also have to call Peláez to come, or to send over a skilled dentist, to check all the dental files here against the cast we've got of the dismembered girl. It's very likely that she was a patient as well.'

SOL

At 12.30 p.m., Elena Fernández had finished her list of dentists, without getting an identification, and had stopped for a coffee in the small bar at the corner of Sol and Carretas before going up to the office to report. She was tired, especially since her father had got her up at 7.30 to go to vote with the rest of the family. She knew he had been torn between two of the parties: the extreme fascists, who saw themselves as Franco's heirs, and the centre-right Unión del Centro Democrático, who were his heirs in fact. Her father's choice of the latter, she felt, was really dictated by his business interests in the construction industry, and she was amused at how he did not doubt that all his family would vote without demur for the party he chose.

As she emerged from the bar refreshed, she was suddenly transfixed at seeing a tall, burly man with a strangely gaunt face, standing on the pavement outside the Gobernación. He was carrying a long parcel wrapped in brown paper, and was staring up at the windows of the DGS building.

I'm sure that's the suspect, Elena said to herself. He's the one the ticket-clerk pointed out to me at Cuatro

Caminos. She wondered what to do. There was hardly
time to go up to the office to alert Navarro. If she
returned to the bar to telephone, the suspect might make
off and she would lose him. She was on the point of
calling the *guardia* standing at the corner of the
Gobernación to arrest the man, when the latter moved off
quickly into the crowd. Elena followed with extreme
nervousness. She had done some shadowing in the
training sessions at the Police School, but this was her first
actual experience of it single-handed.

If she did call a policeman, it would take time to show
him her official badge and persuade him to take action;
the suspect might escape in the resultant confusion. No,
she would shadow him, and when he reached somewhere
definite and looked like staying put for a time, then she
would call in and report. The suspect went down the
stairs into Sol Metro station, and Elena followed, in no
little trepidation.

ALFONSO XIII

At the house in the Avenida de Concha Espina, Varga
had found the likely place where Cortés had stored the
body. 'It's a disused coal-house, chief,' said Varga. 'And
it's damp enough to have caused the formation of
adipocere which Dr Peláez described.'

'What about the clothes?' asked Bernal.

'There's a chest full of very antiquated garments,
dating from 1910 or so, judging by the style. Perhaps the
servant Pilar will be able to tell us whether they've been
here a long time.'

Inspector Quintana came in to tell Bernal that the
dentist's receptionist had arrived.

'Perhaps you'd join Lista and me in questioning her,'

said Bernal. 'We'll do it in her office, where she'll be more at home.'

The receptionist, whose name was Trinidad Juanes, was in her early thirties and wore glasses which hid her natural good looks.

'How long have you worked for Señor Cortés, señorita?' asked Bernal.

'Just two years now, Superintendent,' she replied softly.

'Have you noticed anything strange in his manner recently?'

'Well, yes. For the past two months he's not been himself.' She hesitated. 'At least, not since the nurse left.'

'And why did she leave?'

'I think it was because of what happened with the blonde Portuguese girl who came in for an extraction.'

'When did this occur?'

'In mid-April. She came here one afternoon with severe pain, and the dentist agreed to see her. She wasn't a patient of ours. Señor Cortés's manner was strange; he couldn't keep his eyes off her. I heard him muttering something repeatedly.'

'Was it a name?' asked Bernal.

'Yes, it could have been. The girl only spoke broken Spanish, so I was some time getting her particulars. And all the while he gazed at her, muttering. Quite disturbed, he seemed.'

'As though he thought she was someone else?'

'That's it, Superintendent, you've put your finger on it. As though she was someone he thought he knew, from the past.'

'Could you look up her file?'

'Yes, of course. Sousa was her surname. Let me see . . .' She opened the filing cabinet under S and looked through the cards. 'That's strange, it's gone. I remember typing it out afterwards.'

'Tell us what happened that afternoon.'

'It was a Friday evening, I think. Yes, I'm sure, because I'd arranged to meet my fiancé at 8.30 to go out for a meal. Señor Cortés and the nurse X-rayed Miss Sousa and I heard him tell her she'd have to have a molar extracted. It was the second lower left molar, I think, and he said that the wisdom tooth was impacted against the root of it. He decided to use a local anæsthetic, and asked me to look after her here for ten minutes while it took effect. She was very frightened, and I tried to console her.'

'Then what happened?'

'Well, I wasn't present, but I could hear that Señor Cortés was having difficulty with the extraction. The crown broke and he said he'd have to give the patient a general anæsthetic to cut open the gum. I could hear the nurse arguing with him, but he administered an injection of Pentothal. While they waited for it to take effect, the nurse came out and whispered to me that he was behaving very oddly. She thought he should have sent the girl to the dental hospital.'

'But he persisted in trying to extract the root?'

'Yes, and quite a struggle it was. I could hear him swearing. The Portuguese girl was the last patient, and I was getting ready to leave. Then I heard the nurse exclaim, and she rushed out white-faced. "She's stopped breathing," she said, "and there's no pulse." "Shall I ring for an ambulance?" I asked her. But Señor Cortés followed her out and said, "I think she's all right now, nurse, but you could get Dr Sánchez from the end of the street just in case. There's no need for an ambulance." The nurse put on her coat and rushed out.'

'She didn't go back into the surgery?' asked Bernal.

'No, Superintendent, not then, anyway. Then Señor Cortés told me I could go home, saying the patient was coming out of the anæsthetic quite normally. I was surprised, and offered to stay in case he needed help. Other times he'd asked me to help him walk patients up and down the room to bring them round.'

'So you went. Do you know if the doctor came?'

'I asked the dentist the next day, but he said the doctor hadn't come for twenty minutes and in the meantime Miss Sousa had recovered and he'd taken her into the house and offered her some coffee. He hadn't charged her a fee, considering what had happened.'

'Did you see the nurse the next day?' asked Bernal.

'No, and I haven't seen her since. He sent her what salary was due plus a month's pay in lieu of notice. He said she was a panicker.'

'And did he get another nurse?'

'He's advertised for one, but he says none of them has been suitable so far.'

'So he's been practising alone for two months?'

'Yes, and he does everything himself. It's very strange, really.'

'Perhaps you'll give us the name and address of the nurse who left, señorita, so that we can get in touch with her.'

'Of course,' she said, 'I'll write it down for you.' Bernal passed the card to Lista, who went out with it. 'Could you tell me what all this is about, Superintendent? Has something happened to Señor Cortés?'

'Something has happened to one of the patients, señorita, and so far we can't locate Señor Cortés. Now I want you to look up these names in the files for me.' He read out the names slowly to her. 'Eusebio Flores García. María Luz Cabrera Salazar. Paloma Ledesma Pascual.' One by one she extracted the corresponding cards. 'You note down the date of each visit, I suppose?'

'Oh yes, and the treatment received. Then I send an account, if they're account patients, or they pay on the spot.'

'Could you look at the last date of treatment for each of those three patients?'

'They're all recent, in May and June.'

'After the nurse had left?'

'Yes, that's right.'

'And do you remember those particular patients on those days?'

'Well, I remember Señorita Ledesma. She's been coming here for years, and is always quite friendly. I usually have a chat with her, but during her last visit, which was just for a clean and polish, Señor Cortés sent me out to buy some cotton-wool pads from the chemist's in the Plaza.'

'So you didn't see her leave?'

'No, I didn't.'

'What about Señorita Cabrera?'

'She wanted to have a gold bridge fixed over a gap she had in the left lower premolars. Señor Cortés was arranging to meet her that evening to take her to a specialized dental laboratory for a fitting. He had taken the necessary measurements earlier.'

'Do you remember where he arranged to meet her?'

'In the Calle de Velázquez, I think. It struck me it was a very late hour for such an appointment, but Señor Cortés said the mechanic could only see them then. She would have to come back here for the fixing of the bridge.'

'And Flores?'

'Oh, the *travestí*, you mean? I don't think the dentist noticed, but I filled out his card from the *carnet de identidad*. He just had a small filling.'

'Did you see him leave?'

'Come to think of it, I didn't. I went to make some coffee, and had to go out to buy some beans. He paid before the treatment, because he wasn't a regular patient.'

'Does Señor Cortés always use Pentothal for total anæsthetics and cocaine for local ones?'

'Pentothal, yes, but cocaine hasn't been used for some

years.' Bernal looked troubled. 'It's the substitute, procaine hydrochloride he uses now. I'm sure, because I order the supplies.'

'Are you sure he never uses cocaine?'

'He may still have some in the drugs cupboard. He keeps the key to that.'

'We'll have a look shortly. Tell me, señorita, what is he like to work for?'

'Rather cold and stand-offish. I've never really got to know him. Of course, he's got the old lady there with the servant looking after her, so he's got his problems. But he's a loner. He doesn't seem to have a social life. He spends a lot of time in his workshop in the basement.'

'Have you ever been down there?'

'No, never. I don't think anyone has been. He does sculpture there, I believe.'

SOL

In Bernal's office, Navarro was organizing the all-units search for Roberto Cortés Díaz. He had sent Carlos Miranda and Ángel Gallardo out to Concha Espina to the Superintendent's assistance. He was surprised Elena hadn't reported, although it was past two o'clock. The phone rang and he picked it up.

'Superintendent Bernal's office. This is Inspector Navarro.' He listened for a while. 'I see. That's very good of Traffic Control to find it so quickly. In the underground car-park at the Plaza del Carmen, you say? Very well. Thank you.'

He rang through to Bernal to inform him that Cortés's car had been found.

BILBAO

Elena Fernández was becoming afraid of being spotted by the suspect. She had followed him on to a train going northward on Line 1, but he had alighted at Bilbao station and changed to Line 4, where they were now on the eastbound platform. She was absolutely convinced that this man was the Metro murderer and wondered what he was carrying in the long package. She shuddered, and felt sick as she thought what it might be. She had watched carefully to make sure he didn't leave it in the train or on a platform seat.

There weren't many people on the platform, so she kept well away from the suspect and pretended to study the Metro plan on the wall, while watching him out of the corner of her eye. When the train arrived, he made no move to board it, and she wondered if he would notice that she also would remain behind when it departed. But he didn't appear to spare a glance for her. Instead he examined all the carriages nearest to him and got in at the last moment. She managed to jump into the next carriage to his just as the doors were closing.

ALFONSO XIII

By 2.15 p.m., Bernal was questioning the dentist's former nurse, who had been tracked to a dentist in Ciudad Lineal. Inspector Quintana had gone to collect her in his car.

Asunción Mora looked pale and worried in Bernal's presence.

'Could you tell me why you left Señor Cortés's employ?'

'It was his extraordinary behaviour, Superintendent. Most of the time he acted quite normally, very calmly in fact, even when things went slightly wrong. Some dentists panic, you know. But two months ago he did an emergency extraction for a Portuguese girl and I thought his behaviour very peculiar.'

'In what way, señorita?'

'First, he gave her a general anæsthetic on top of a local one of procaine, for an extraction he couldn't hope to complete successfully, so far as I could see. The root was jammed by an impacted third molar, and it was a hospital job, I was sure. But he seemed to become quite manic, determined not to be defeated by it. I was watching the patient's breathing and pulse, and suddenly both stopped. I was convinced she had died, and ran out to telephone for an ambulance. But he sent me instead to fetch Dr Sánchez, who lives down the hill, and he said he'd started giving oxygen and she was coming round. The doctor was out, but was expected back at any moment. I returned with him, but when we got here the patient had left.'

'Did he explain what had happened?'

'He said he'd taken her to the house and given her coffee. When she'd recovered, she went home. I found it hard to believe at first, but I admit I panicked when her heart stopped beating. I didn't think it would be possible to revive her. Anyway, I was frightened and asked for my cards, which he gave me without making a fuss. He even sent me an extra month's salary.'

'Was this the only bad experience you had while you were working here?'

'Yes, but it was enough.'

GOYA

Elena watched the suspect through the windows at the end of the carriage as the train proceeded eastward on

Line 4. At one point she thought he had begun to unwrap the parcel he was carrying, but her view was partly obscured by a young girl who was standing in front of him. She noticed how wildly he was staring at the girl, and Elena became frightened for her. She felt in her handbag for her small service revolver. But the suspect alighted at Goya, and she got out and walked away from him down the platform, certain he would spot her shadowing him. Stopping to look at a wall-poster, she noticed that he had sat down on a bench, and was attending to his parcel.

Taking a sudden decision, she marched into the station-master's glass-panelled office and showed him her official badge. 'Would you allow me to use the outside telephone?'

'Of course, Inspectora.'

She dialled the DGS number and asked for Bernal's office. There was a delay. 'Is there another train due immediately?' she asked the station-master.

'In three minutes, if it's on time.'

'What number will it be?'

'Number twenty-eight.'

Navarro came on the line.

'Paco, this is Elena. I spotted the suspect in Sol on the way to the office. He's carrying a long package. I've followed him here to Goya station, where he's sitting on a bench on Line 4 northbound platform. We've already been on two trains, having come via Bilbao. The next train due here is number twenty-eight, northbound.'

'Stick with him, Elena, but on no account approach him. He's very dangerous. He's a dentist called Roberto Cortés Díaz, and the chief is going over his house at the moment in Concha Espina. You should find a *gris* on most platforms. Call one of them to help you if he does anything violent. Be careful, now, and phone in when you can.'

'The train is coming, Paco. I'll call you again.'

SOL

Navarro got in touch with Bernal at once and told him of Elena's initiative.

'I'm coming in at once, Paco, to direct the search. Let's hope she's following the right man. I'll send some men down to train number twenty-eight, since they're coming in this direction.'

GOYA

Elena looked out of the office window as the train drew in. But the suspect didn't get up from the platform seat. She noticed he no longer held the package, but had folded the wrapping-paper up on the seat beside him. After the train departed, he rose and made for the exit, under the sign that said 'Correspondencia Línea 2: Ventas—Cuatro Caminos'. So he was going to change lines once more. And she had no time to phone in again.

Keeping a discreet distance behind him, she noticed he was holding something bulky under his raincoat.

ALFONSO XIII

Bernal, more and more alarmed by Elena's plight, sent Miranda and Lista in a car to Alfonso XIII station to meet train number twenty-eight, while Inspector Quintana rang his District Comisaría in the Calle de Cartagena and ordered some of his uniformed men to go down to Cartagena station, which was an intermediate station on the route. At least Elena would see the *grises* and call them if she needed help.

Meanwhile Bernal took Angel Gallardo back with him in the official car to Sol. As they were leaving, the servant-woman approached Bernal nervously. 'I've noticed that something is missing from the wall in the gallery, Superintendent, where Don Roberto has a collection of Civil War relics.'

'What is it, Pilar? What has he got?'

'A bayonet,' she said nervously. 'I've just noticed the blank space between the other weapons.'

'Are all the guns there?'

'Yes, I think so. It's only the bayonet that's missing.'

'Thank you, Pilar, we'll attend to it. Don't worry, now.'

When they drove away, Bernal spoke to Navarro on the car radio. 'Did Elena say the suspect was carrying a long package? Over.'

'Yes, chief. He still had it at Goya station when she called. Over.'

'It probably contains a Civil War bayonet—yes, a bayonet—so things look grim. Let's hope she doesn't try to tackle him. Warn her as soon as she phones in. Over and out.'

GOYA

Elena followed the suspect cautiously, allowing other travellers to come between them in the passageways and staircases between Lines 4 and 2. She hurried a little to see whether Cortés took the stairs to the westbound or eastbound trains. Ah, westbound, direction Ópera and Cuatro Caminos. He was going round in a circle, she realized. Was he trying to shake her off, or was he wandering aimlessly from station to station?

She kept wondering what he had hidden under his commando-type raincoat. She hoped it wasn't anything gruesome. But if it was, why had he unwrapped it? She started to think it might be a weapon of some sort. What could it be? It was clearly far too short to be a rifle, and too long to be a pistol, even with a silencer. A sawn-off shot-gun? It didn't seem bulky enough.

She debated whether to risk telephoning once more. He was sitting down again on a platform seat with his head lowered. He hadn't given the impression of looking round to see if anyone was following him. Just then a westbound train could be heard approaching. She was nearest the train and watched for the cardboard square bearing its number in the driver's cab. Number forty-three. Perhaps she'd get a chance to telephone from another station.

But the suspect made no attempt to board the train. The whistle blew and the doors closed. She decided to mingle with the passengers who had alighted and pass the murderer, in order to get to the station-master's office.

SOL

When he arrived at his office, Bernal received the reports from Cartagena and Alfonso XIII stations: there was no sign of Elena and the suspect on train number twenty-eight on Line 4, nor had they been spotted at the intermediary stations. He and Navarro studied the large wall-plan of the Metro system.

'We'll call Miranda and Lista in. We may need them here. You realize, Paco, that at Goya the killer may have changed his mind and taken Line 2 in either direction,' said Bernal. 'Perhaps he's cottoned on to the fact that he's being followed. Let's get on to the Metro Director and see if he can give us a direct line to Sol Central Control. We could even stop the service for a while, if necessary, while we search the trains and stations.'

'If only we could let Elena know what he's armed with, chief,' said Ángel, who had come over to study the map.

Navarro was speaking urgently to the Metropolitan Company. 'The Director would like to speak to you, chief.'

GOYA

Elena was about to enter the station-master's office to report in, when she saw the suspect get up slowly from the seat, with the air of someone who had come to a decision. He glanced up and down the platform, and she hastily turned to read the official notices stuck on the windows of the office. She could hear a train approaching. Number forty-four, westbound, she calculated.

She risked a glance to see if the suspect intended boarding it. Yes, it looked as though he did. He was still keeping one hand inside the fold of his raincoat lapel, presumably in order to support the object he was hiding. What on earth could it be, she wondered. It looked heavy. A dagger? It was too big to be that.

SOL

'I've got full authority to suspend the service on any line should the need arise,' Bernal told his two colleagues. 'You'll have an open line to Sol Control in a few moments, Paco.'

'But will it put Elena and other passengers in more danger if we have the power cut off, chief? If he is trapped in a tunnel in the dark, he might go berserk with that bayonet,' objected Paco.

'You're probably right,' admitted Bernal. 'If only we had direct contact with Elena on a two-way radio.'

'It might not work from the underground,' said Ángel. 'Surely she'll try to phone in when she has the opportunity. She'll realize we think she was on Line 4 going northwards.'

BANCO

Again Elena had entered the carriage next to the suspect's and observed him through the end-windows of the two coaches. There were more people now, which made her task seem easier. She also took the chance of undoing her hair, which had been pinned up, and of taking off her thin tweed jacket and putting it back on inside out. Fortunately it was reversible, and was plain pale green on the inner side. She remembered from her training that these tiny changes often sufficed to disguise someone shadowing a suspect.

Once more she noticed that her quarry moved to stand behind a young girl, whom he stared at strangely. As the train swayed into Banco station, she thought he was about to attack the girl, but the movement stopped, and he assumed his former posture, leaning against the carriage window. He was so close to her she could have touched him if it weren't for the glass divisions between the carriages.

SOL

At Sol station the suspect got off in the crush, and Elena followed closely, afraid of losing him in the busiest of all the stations. But he stopped at the first platform-seat and sat down once more. Walking boldly past him she made for the telephone in the station-master's office. She fumed while this official examined her credentials, after which he reluctantly allowed her to use the telephone.

'Paco, this is Elena. I'm just below you at Sol station, on the westbound platform of Line 2. We've just got off train number forty-four, and the suspect is sitting on a bench.'

'Hold on, here's the chief.'

'Elena? Stay where you are. I'm sending Ángel down to you with two plainclothesmen. The man you are following is Roberto Cortés, an insane dentist, and he's armed with a bayonet — a war relic. Don't approach him, do you hear?'

'Yes, chief, but what if he makes off before Ángel arrives? Train number forty-five is due on this line at any moment.'

'Follow him discreetly if he gets on it. Remember he may change to Line 1 or to Line 3, or, of course, go back eastwards on Line 2. My hunch is he'll go to Line 1. That's where his sister was killed in 1939.'

'In 1939?' Elena echoed. 'What's that got to do with it?'

'Everything. He's a psychopath. That's the memory that triggers his present actions.'

'The train's coming,' she said urgently.

'Look out and see if he moves. I'll hold on. If you don't come back to talk to me within a minute, I'll assume you've followed him on to the train and I'll get Metro Control to cut off the power on Line 2 until Ángel arrives.'

Elena peered anxiously along the platform. No, the murderer hadn't moved. He sat motionless, his head bowed, gazing at the floor. The whistle blew and the train doors closed. He wasn't travelling on that one. She rushed back to the phone.

'He's still there. He hasn't moved from the bench.'

'Very well. Stay there and observe him until Ángel arrives with the plainclothesmen.'

When she returned to the doorway, Elena was horrified to see that the killer had disappeared. She looked up and down the platform—which way had he gone? She read the sign over the exit nearest to where he'd been sitting: *Correspondencia Línea 1, Portazgo—Plaza de Castilla.* That was the line Bernal had the hunch about. She went quickly along the passageway and up the stairs to the busy hallway, which was nearly ankle deep in election propaganda. Still no sign of him. By heaven, he'd moved much more quickly than before. Had he spotted her shadowing him? At the entrance to Line 1 she hesitated; the northbound or southbound platform? The northbound stairs was nearer, so she took it. In any case she might still see him on the opposite platform if he'd taken the other stairs.

She ran down the staircase just as a train whistled, and suddenly saw Cortés boarding it. She managed to beat the automatic barrier that closed off the stairway immediately prior to the departure of a train, sprinted across the platform and squeezed through the doors as they were closing. The train was very full, and she realized she was only a few feet from the murderer. She turned her back on him to face the doors.

Ángel Gallardo was horrified not to find Elena on Line 2 westbound platform. He rushed into the office and asked the station-master where Inspectora Fernández had gone.

'It beats me,' he said. 'It's like a madhouse here this afternoon. She put down the phone and rushed out as train number forty-five left, and she didn't come back.'

'Did she get on the train?'

'I don't see how she could have. The doors were closed. Now Central Control has just sent a general warning that the power may be cut at any moment.'

'That's for us, if we need it,' said Ángel. 'Come on,' he said to the two plainclothesmen. 'Let's go to Line 1 and follow the chief's hunch.'

They got to the northbound platform to find their way barred by the automatic barrier. Peering through the mesh at the side, Ángel caught a glimpse of Elena's pale face as the train departed.

JOSÉ ANTONIO

On the short run uphill from Sol to José Antonio, Elena felt someone pressing close behind her. Oh God, let it not be the psychopath, she prayed, cautiously opening her handbag with the hand that held it, while clinging to the support bar near the door with the other. Then she felt something sharp in the middle of her back.

SOL

When the automatic barrier opened, Ángel stormed into the station-master's office on Line 1, waving his DGS badge.

'What number was that train?'

'Number fifty-two,' replied the astonished official.

'Let me use the phone.' Ángel dialled the number. 'Superintendent? It's Ángel. She followed him on to train number fifty-two on Line 1, northbound. We were trapped by the automatic barrier. What shall we do?'

'Come back here and take an official car. Make for Tribunal. I'll hold that train at José Antonio for a while to give you more time. Contact me by radio as soon as you're mobile.'

JOSÉ ANTONIO

When the train stopped at José Antonio and the doors opened, Elena tried to get out with other passengers who were alighting, but she felt a powerful arm circling her waist, and the man whispered in her ear, 'Stay just where you are,' and he pressed the point of the bayonet into her back until it pierced the skin.

She wondered whether to scream and surprise him, or to bring out the pistol, but she was hardly in a position to turn it on him. She noticed that the train remained on the platform with the doors open for much longer than usual, but no policeman came by, and in any case she would get stabbed before he or anyone else could come to her aid. She tried to calculate the possibilities of using the karate she had been taught, but there would hardly be room to carry it through, since many more passengers had now entered the carriage.

Some of the passengers began to comment on the delay, and she felt the bayonet press harder. Finally the doors closed and the train moved off. One or two passengers looked at Elena and the suspect curiously. No doubt they thought they were an engaged couple, to be embracing so closely in public. Elena remembered it was a long run to the next station, Tribunal. Should she try reasoning with him? Wouldn't he have expected her to protest, unless he'd realized she was a policewoman who had been following him? Oh God, what a predicament. She half-turned her head and muttered, 'What the hell do you want?'

'Shut up, or it'll be the worse for you.' He pressed the bayonet harder, until it pierced the flesh, and she clenched her teeth in pain.

SOL

Bernal screamed orders into the telephone. 'I want that train to leave José Antonio now, do you understand? Don't cut the current when it's in the tunnel. It would be far too dangerous. Stop it at Tribunal. Yes, yes. Would it be possible to cut the power just as it stops at the platform, before the doors are opened? You must try. That should give my men time to reach the station.'

Perspiring heavily, he turned to Paco. 'Has Ángel come in on the radio yet?'

'Yes, I've just got him.'

'Turn on the big loudspeaker so I can hear him.' He picked up the microphone. 'Ángel, can you hear me? Over.'

'Loud and clear, chief. We're half way up Hortaleza, but the traffic is quite heavy. Over.'

'Make for Tribunal station. I'm going to hold the train there with the doors shut and the power off until you get there. As fast as you can, now. Over.'

'We'll cut through Mejía Lequerica and along Barceló. Over.'

'I've ordered the local Comisaría to post uniformed men to stop the public entering Tribunal station. Over and out.'

TRIBUNAL

Train number fifty-two swayed as it accelerated towards Tribunal station, but Elena's hopes of freeing herself were dashed when the psychopath clutched her waist even more tightly. She was afraid she'd get a serious stab wound simply from the motion of the train. She debated whether to start screaming at Tribunal, where there should be a policeman on the platform. She felt the brakes coming on, and the train slowed. The platform lights came into sight. She kept perfectly still, waiting for the doors to open, intending to make a quick karate movement as the other passengers moved.

When the train stopped, all the carriage lights went out and the doors remained shut. Those passengers intending to alight exclaimed in surprise. 'What's happening?' asked a small man in front of Elena. 'I've never known this to happen before.' She gave him a desperate smile, and he glanced inquisitively at the burly man restraining her. The loudspeakers along the platform crackled, and the station-master made an announcement. 'We have a temporary break in the current. Please be patient and do not panic.'

It's Bernal's doing, thought Elena. He's arranged this. She felt a little more cheerful, waiting to see how the psychopath reacted. She saw a grey-uniformed policeman walk by, looking idly into the carriages. The murderer stiffened, and pressed the bayonet harder. She bit her lip. Two or three minutes passed. The few people on the platform waved at the trapped passengers. 'Don't worry,' shouted a cheerful woman, 'they'll soon have the power on again.'

Suddenly Elena saw Ángel approaching slowly along the platform, followed by two plainclothesmen whose faces she recognized. She tried to control her feeling of relief so that the killer wouldn't sense it through his close contact with her. Ángel passed the carriage, appearing to glance idly in, and gave no sign of recognition, but he stopped quite soon afterwards, without proceeding along the length of the train. She was hopeful that he had spotted her. Then out of the corner of her eye, she saw a posse of *grises*, and hoped the murderer hadn't seen them, or he might panic.

Without warning the carriage lights came on and the

doors opened, and Ángel and the plainclothesmen made a rush for her and the psychopath, knocking them both sideways to the ground. The women in the carriage screamed. Elena was pulled away, and she rolled under a seat. Cortés struggled to his feet and brandished the bayonet, causing the women to scream more loudly, and he made for the doors, forced his way through the uniformed men and ran along the platform. One of the *grises* drew his gun and fired a number of times, creating a general panic, but Ángel ordered him to desist. Cortés disappeared past the driver's cab down the steps into the tunnel.

Ángel helped Elena on to the platform, examining the bloodstain on the back of her jacket. 'Are you hurt?'

'Only a surface wound. I don't think it's deep,' she managed to reply.

'We'll get you first aid.'

'Why don't you go after him?'

'He'll not get far. Our men are in close pursuit.'

Bernal arrived at that moment mopping his brow with a handkerchief. 'Thank God, you're all right, Elena. Did he wound you?'

'Only a scratch, I think, chief.'

'We'll take you to a doctor. Where is he, Ángel?'

'He's run off into the tunnel.'

'Have you held the trains and cut off the current while we search?'

'I haven't had time to yet.'

'Did he have a gun, Elena?' asked Bernal.

'I don't think so. Only the bayonet.'

Just then there was the sound of a train approaching from the north and a sudden scream of terror.

'My God, I hope it wasn't one of our men,' said Bernal anxiously. 'I'll get the current cut off.'

Later, when the track was searched, all the policemen having been accounted for, the mangled remains of

Roberto Cortés Díaz were discovered under the wheels of train number fifty-six, southbound.

SOL

Later that day, after Elena had been bandaged by a doctor and taken home to recuperate, Bernal dictated a full report for the judge of instruction. Navarro helped him to assemble the forensic and technical reports they had received, and they attached copies to the main report.

'Paco, you'd better contact the Portuguese National Police, and send them the fingerprints and dental cast of Miss Sousa. It's a very common surname in Portugal, and they'll have a job to identify her and trace her relatives. We'd better get in touch with Cortés's eldest brother, for him to take responsibility for the old lady, and for making the funeral arrangements.'

'Very well, chief. I told the rest of the group they could go home. This has been a hard slog.'

'I'll go and see the Subsecretary now and ask him to arrange for Elena to receive an official commendation. He'll also want to prepare a statement for the press. If you've time, we could meet for a drink afterwards.'

ANTÓN MARTÍN

At 8 p.m. Bernal and Navarro were sipping large *jarras* of beer in the Cervecería Alemana, looking out at the children playing noisily in the Plaza de Santa Ana in the gathering dusk.

'What I don't understand, chief, is what triggered off

Cortés to commit these crimes after all those years.'

'I think it may have been fortuitous,' said Bernal. 'The Portuguese girl happened to remind him of his dead sister. Through nervousness he committed professional negligence and she died in his surgery, so he took his chance and hid the body in his cellar, pretending that she had left the premises. Then later he destroyed the record card his secretary had made out. He must have felt safe from discovery, since she was a foreign national. It could well be that until that fateful afternoon he had only fantasized with the mannequins he made out of plastic.'

'And why did he put two of the mannequins in the Metro, after the Portuguese girl's death?'

'Trial runs, I think, to see if he could get away with it. In the meantime, of course, her corpse had putrefied, and was unsuitable for carrying into the Underground to recreate that obsessional image. So he dismembered it, in order to dispose of it piece by piece.'

'Why did he choose the other three victims in particular, out of all his patients?' asked Navarro.

'A question of opportunity, perhaps, though they were all fair-haired, and the Ledesma and Cabrera girls bore some resemblance to his sister. He had no nurse there by then, but he had to send the receptionist out on some pretext each time. He had an old stock of cocaine, so it was easy to inject the victims with a large overdose. Apart from that, I suppose they had to be dressed like his dead sister, and generally made to fit his mental picture of the scene. He only slipped up with the *travestí*.' Bernal lit another Kaiser. 'Let's have another jar of this beer, Paco, and some *tapas* to line our stomachs.'

RETIRO

On his way home that night, Bernal passed the lines of presiding officers, queueing outside the Escuela Aguirre in the Calle de Alcalá to hand in the returns for each electoral table.

He found Eugenia glued to the television set. 'I've made you an omelette, and warmed up some pork chops, Luis. Do you think the reds are going to take over this country?'

'I doubt it somehow, Geñita. Have they given any news yet?'

'No, but they promise a projection from the first results shortly.'

Bernal poured himself a large glass of the red wine she had brought from the country. The strident music of the *Telediario* came on. The announcer gave the first computer prediction: '*It seems that the UCD—the centre right party of the Government—will have the largest number of votes, and therefore of seats, both in the Congress of Deputies and in the Senate. The PSOE—the socialist party—will form the second largest group.*'

'There you are, Geñita,' said Luis. 'It won't be like 1936 at all.'

'I hope you're right, Luis, but poor Señor Blas Piñar has come out badly.'

The announcer went on to other national news. '*Line One of the Madrid Metro was halted for a time this afternoon, while units of the Brigada Criminal searched for the Metro murderer. He was killed in a tunnel at Tribunal station by an oncoming train while trying to evade arrest. This successful police operation was led by Superintendent Luis Bernal and his Group.*'

'Oh, Luis,' moaned Eugenia. 'They've mentioned you again! Whatever will my relatives in Ciudad Rodrigo be thinking of us?'